## "All right. What's the plan?"

"A night off. With me. You put on your best party dress, let me take you out to dinner. You talk about yourself, not the things you're supposed to be doing. You let me take responsibility for showing you a good time. You relax. We have a nightcap in my suite, then you get a good night's sleep."

"In my own room?" Luce stamped down on the corner of her mind that was happily imagining what might happen if they were both in his room.

Ben's smile grew a little wolfish. "Well now, that's up to you."

"Really," Luce said, flatly.

"Of course." Ben looked mildly offended. "I'm not saying I won't give it my best shot. You're a beautiful woman, and I enjoy the company of beautiful women. But at the end of the night, you get the choice of my bed or the spare room. Either way you have a bed for the night."

Luce found her gaze caught on his. He thought she was beautiful? Ben Hampton actually wanted her. Sober, all grown up, not obviously crazy…and he wanted her. She could have dinner with him, flirt, kiss…more. All she had to do was say yes.

**Dear Reader**

There's something magical about snow. Especially when you're sitting inside by a warm fire, mug in hand, watching it fall and cover the land. Or crunching through the first fall, leaving crisp footprints in your wake. Building snowmen, sledging, running inside to warm up again...or just enjoying the hush that a good snowfall brings to the world.

Of course if you're trying to drive through mid-Wales in a snowstorm, like Luce and Ben are in this book, it's a whole lot less fun. Especially if it traps you in a cottage in the middle of nowhere with someone you haven't seen in ten years and didn't like very much even then.

But the magic of snow can't be resisted, and the power of a romantic, secluded cottage shouldn't be underestimated. Until the inevitable thaw, when the world returns to normal—but leaves Ben and Luce changed for ever...

I grew up on the Welsh border—not very far from Chester, where this story starts—and I had so much fun setting this book in familiar locations. Ben's cottage is, I'm afraid, fictional, but based on many cottages I've spent very happy holidays in over the years. And while the restaurant where they first eat dinner together doesn't exist in the real world, the one that sits in the same spot on the Chester Rows in reality is a favourite for Mum and me to stop at for lunch when indulging in a little retail therapy!

I hope you enjoy Ben and Luce's snowy adventure— maybe even as much as I enjoyed writing it.

Best wishes

*Sophie*

# STRANDED WITH THE TYCOON

BY
SOPHIE PEMBROKE

First published in Great Britain 2013
by Mills & Boon, an imprint of Harlequin (UK) Limited.
Harlequin (UK) Limited, Eton House, 18-24 Paradise Road,
Richmond, Surrey TW9 1SR

© Sophie Pembroke 2013

ISBN: 978 0 263 23548 7

Harlequin (UK) policy is to use papers that are natural, renewable and recyclable products and made from wood grown in sustainable forests. The logging and manufacturing process conform to the legal environmental regulations of the country of origin.

Printed and bound in Great Britain
by CPI Antony Rowe, Chippenham, Wiltshire

**Sophie Pembroke** has been dreaming, reading and writing romance for years—ever since she first read *The Far Pavilions* under her desk in Chemistry class. She later stayed up all night devouring Harlequin® Mills & Boon books as part of her English degree at Lancaster University, and promptly gave up any pretext of enjoying tragic novels. After all, what's the point of a book without a happy ending?

She loves to set her novels in the places where she has lived—from the wilds of the Welsh mountains to the genteel humour of an English country village, or the heat and tension of a London summer. She also has a tendency to make her characters kiss in castles.

Currently Sophie makes her home in Hertfordshire, with her scientist husband (who still shakes his head at the reading-in-Chemistry thing) and their four-year-old *Alice-in-Wonderland*-obsessed daughter. She writes her love stories in the study she begrudgingly shares with her husband, while drinking too much tea and eating homemade cakes. Or, when things are looking very bad for her heroes and heroines, white wine and dark chocolate.

Sophie keeps a blog at www.SophiePembroke.com, which should be about romance and writing but is usually about cake and castles instead.

*This is Sophie Pembroke's fabulous first book
for Mills & Boon® Romance!*

For Holly.
I'm proud of you all the way to the moon, too.

# CHAPTER ONE

Lucinda Myles wasn't the sort of woman to panic, usually. But the prospect of being without a bed for the night five days before Christmas, in the midst of the coldest December the north-west of England had seen in decades, was decidedly unappealing. The city of Chester was booked solid by Christmas shoppers and by the other unfortunate academics attending the badly timed *Bringing History to the Future* conference. If the Royal Court Hotel didn't find her booking…well, she was going to need a new plan. But first she'd try dogged persistence. It had always worked for her grandfather.

'I understand that you're fully booked,' Luce said, in her most patient and forbearing voice. The one she usually saved for her brother Tom, when he was being particularly obtuse. 'But one of those room bookings should be for me. Dr Lucinda Myles.' She leant across the reception desk to try to see the girl's computer screen. 'M-Y-L-E-S.'

The blonde behind the desk angled the screen away from her. 'I'm afraid there is no booking at this hotel under that name for tonight. Or any other night, for that matter.'

Luce gritted her teeth. This was what she got for letting the conference staff take charge of her hotel booking. She really should have known better. *Take responsibility.*

*Take control.* Words to live by, her grandfather had always said. Shame she was the only one in the family to listen.

As if to echo the thought, her phone buzzed in her pocket. Luce sighed as she reached in to dig it out, knowing without looking that it would be Tom. 'And there are absolutely no free rooms in the hotel tonight?' she asked the blonde, figuring it was worth one more shot. 'Even the suites are booked?' She could make the university reimburse her. They wanted her here at the conference— the least they could do was give her a decent room for the night.

'Everything. Every room is booked. It's Christmas, in case you hadn't noticed. And now, if I can't be of any further assistance…' The blonde looked over Luce's shoulder.

Glancing back herself, Luce saw a growing queue of people waiting to check in. Well, they were just going to have to wait. She wasn't going to be intimidated by this fancy hotel with its marble floors, elegant golden Christmas tree, chandeliers and impatient businessmen. She'd had one hell of a day, and she was taking responsibility for making it better. 'Actually, perhaps you could check if any of the other local hotels have a free room. Since you've lost my reservation.'

'We haven't—' the blonde started, but Luce cut her off with a look. She sighed. 'I'll just check.'

While the blonde motioned to her colleague to come and assist with the check-in queue, Luce slid a finger across the touch screen of her phone to check her messages. Three texts and a voicemail. All in the last twenty minutes, while she'd been arguing with the receptionist. A light day, really.

She scrolled to the first text while the disgruntled businessman behind her checked in at the next computer. It was from Tom, of course.

*Has Mum spoken to you about Christmas Eve? Can you do it?*

Christmas Eve? Luce frowned. That meant the voice-mail was probably from her mother, changing their festive plans for the sixth time that month.

The next text was from her sister Dolly.

*Looking forward to Xmas Eve—especially chocolate pots!*

That didn't bode well. Christmas Day was planned and sorted and all due for delivery from the local supermarket on the twenty-third—apart from the turkey, which was safely stored in her freezer. Christmas Eve, however— that was a whole different proposition.

The final text was Tom again.

*Mum says we have a go! Fantastic. See you then.*

Luce sighed. Whatever Mum's new plan was, apparently it was a done deal. 'You're the responsible one, Lucinda,' her grandfather had always said. 'The rest of them couldn't take care of themselves for a minute out there in the real world. You and I know that. Which is why you're going to have to do it for them.'

Apparently they needed looking after again. With a Christmas Eve dinner. And chocolate puddings. Presumably in addition to the three-course dinner she'd be expected to produce the following day. Perfect.

Luce clicked the phone off as the blonde came back. The voicemail from her mother, hopefully explaining everything, could wait until Luce had a bed for the night.

'I'm sorry,' the blonde said, without a hint of apology

in her voice. 'There's some history conference in town, and with all the Christmas shoppers as well I'm afraid the local accommodation has been booked up for months.'

*Of course it has,* Luce wanted to say. *I'm here for the damn conference. I booked my room months ago. I've just spent all morning discussing how to bring history into the future. I deserve a room.*

But instead she clenched her jaw while she thought her way out of the problem.

'Right, then,' she said after a moment. 'I'm going to go and sit over there and try calling some places myself.' She motioned to the bar at the side of the lobby, where discreet twinkling fairy lights beckoned. This day would definitely be better with a gin and tonic. 'In the meantime, if you have any cancellations, I'd appreciate it if you'd book the room under my name.'

'Of course.' The blonde nodded, but her tone said, *You'll be lucky.*

Sighing, Luce turned away from the desk, only to find her path to a G&T barred by a broad chest in an expensive shirt. A nice chest. A wide, warm chest. The sort of chest you could bury your face in and forget about your day and let the owner of the chest solve your problems instead.

Not that she needed a man to fix her problems, of course. She was perfectly capable of doing that herself, thank you.

But it would be nice if one offered, just once.

Raising her gaze, she saw that the chest was topped by an almost unbelievably good-looking face. Dark hair brushed back from tanned skin. Golden-brown eyes that glowed above an amused mouth. A small scar marring his left eyebrow.

Hang on. That scar was familiar. She knew this man. And she should probably stop staring.

'Is there a problem with your reservation, madam?' he asked, and Luce blinked.

'Um, only that it doesn't seem to exist.' She glanced back at the reception desk to discover that the blonde, rather than assisting the next guest in the queue, was practically hanging over the counter to get in on their conversation.

'Daisy?' The man raised his scarred eyebrow at the blonde.

Luce definitely recognised that expression. But from where? A conference? A lecture? Somebody's ex? Hell, maybe even from TV? One of those reality shows about real life in a hotel? Except Luce didn't usually have time to watch such programmes. But the subconscious was a funny thing. Maybe his image had been imprinted on her brain, somehow, in eerie preparation for this moment.

'There's no reservation in her name, sir, and the hotel's fully booked tonight. I tried the usual places, of course, but everyone's booked out.'

For the first time Daisy sounded helpful and efficient. Obviously this guy was someone who mattered. Or Daisy had a huge crush on him. Or, most likely, both. After all, Luce could tell from the way he stood—feet apart, just enough to anchor him firmly to the earth—that this was a man used to the world bending around him rather than the other way round. And really, even with the scar—especially with the scar, actually—what young, healthy, straight woman wouldn't feel a certain *ping* of attraction to him?

Except Luce, of course. She had too many bigger things to worry about to waste time on attraction. Like where she was going to sleep that night. And who the hell he was.

Luce frowned. So annoying. Normally she was good at this stuff. Of course the man hadn't given any indication that he recognised *her*, so maybe she was wrong. Or just less memorable than he was.

Suddenly Luce was rather glad she couldn't put her finger on his identity. How much more embarrassing would it be to have to explain to him how he knew her while he stared at her blankly? Much better to get this whole interaction over with quickly. She'd probably figure out where she knew him from when she was on the train back to Cardiff on Thursday morning, by which time it wouldn't matter anyway.

'What about the King James Suite?' he asked.

Luce was amused to see Daisy actually blush.

'Well, I didn't think... I mean...' she stammered.

Luce, seeing her chance, jumped in. 'You thought I couldn't afford it?' she guessed. 'Firstly, you really shouldn't make such assumptions about your guests. Secondly, since you lost my reservation I'd expect that a free upgrade would be the least you could do. So I'm very interested to hear your response to the gentleman's question.'

Arms folded across her chest, just like her grandfather used to do when he was disappointed in her, Luce stared Daisy down and waited for an answer. This was it, she was sure. The moment her luck turned for the day and she got to spend the night in the best luxury the Royal Court Hotel had to offer. Never mind the gin and tonic—she was having champagne in the bathtub at this rate.

Daisy, redder and more flustered than ever, turned wide blue eyes on her boss. 'But, Mr Hampton, sir...I didn't offer her the King James Suite because *you're* staying there.'

Mr Hampton. Ben Hampton. The memory fell into place just as Daisy's words registered.

Luce winced. Apparently her day wasn't improving after all.

* * *

Ben Hampton couldn't keep from smirking when he saw his potential suite-mate roll her eyes to heaven and turn folded arms and an accusing stare on him. This was going to be fun.

Five minutes earlier he'd been about to head out for the evening when he'd seen the brunette holding up the reservations queue in the lobby. His first instinct had been to intervene, to get things moving again. Being one half of the 'sons' in the Hampton & Sons hotel chain meant that he fixed things wherever he saw them. He kept the guests happy, the staff working hard and the hotel ticking over, wherever he happened to be staying at the time. That was his job: keep things moving. Including himself. But of course staff evaluation was also important, his brother Seb would have said, and this had looked like the perfect opportunity to observe how the Royal Court's reception staff dealt with a difficult guest.

So he'd stayed back, trying not to look as if he was loitering behind the ostentatious golden Christmas tree in the lobby, and watched. He'd heard the woman give her name as Lucinda Myles and a jolt of recognition had stabbed through him. Lucinda Myles. *Luce.* They'd teased her about that, hadn't they? Such an absurd nickname for someone so uptight. Ben knew from six months of dating her university roommate that Luce Myles had been the twenty-year-old most likely to be doing extra course reading on a Friday night, while the rest of them were in the pub. And he'd been able to tell from three metres away that she was still the most tightly wound person he'd ever met.

Luce had vibrated with irritation and impatience, just as she had whenever he and the girlfriend had emerged from their bed at noon on a weekday. Ben frowned. What had her name been, anyway? The girlfriend? Molly? Mandy?

Hell, it *had* been eight years ago—even if six months was something of a relationship record for him. Was he supposed to remember the name of every girl he'd ever dated? But Luce Myles...that wholly inaccurate name had stuck with him down the years.

Casually, he'd turned his head to get a better look at her. Dark hair, clipped at the back of her head, had revealed the creamy curve of her neck down to her collarbone, shoulders, tense under her sweater. The heel of her boot had been tapping against the marble as she waited for Daisy to finish calling around for a room Ben knew wouldn't exist. She'd been knotted so tight she might have snapped at any moment, and he'd wondered why—passing acquaintance aside—he was even vaguely interested in her. Yes, he liked a woman who knew what she wanted, but usually she wanted a good time—and him. Lucinda Myles didn't look as if she'd gained any conception of what a good time was in the last decade, let alone a desire to have one.

In fact, he'd realised with a jolt, he knew exactly what she looked like. That permanent frown etched in her forehead, the frustration around her eyes—they were familiar. He'd seen them on his mother's face often enough.

But that hadn't explained his sudden interest. He'd studied her closer and eventually decided it was her clothes. Despite the 'stay away' vibes her demeanour gave out, her clothes were just begging to be touched. Straight velvet skirt in the darkest plum, a navy sweater that looked so soft it had to be cashmere. Even her sensible brown boots were suede. She certainly hadn't dressed like that at university. Ben appreciated fine fabrics, and the sight had made his fingers itch to touch them.

He'd wondered what she had on underneath.

A woman couldn't wear clothes that strokeable if she didn't have something of a sensual nature under them.

Even if she didn't know it was there yet. Maybe Lucinda Myles had an inner sensuality just begging to be let out after all these years. Ben had thought he might like to help her with that. For old times' sake.

Daisy had returned to report on the utter lack of available hotel rooms in the local area, and Luce had moved away—which simply didn't fit in with Ben's plans. So he'd stepped forward and suggested the King James Suite, which had had the added bonus of enabling him to watch Luce's face when she realised who she'd be sharing with.

Except her reaction wasn't quite what he'd been expecting.

There'd been no sign that she recognised him, for a start, which was a bit of a blow to the ego. He liked to think he was a fairly memorable guy. But then, he'd grown up in eight years. Changed just as she had. Would he have recognised her without hearing her name? Probably not. So he could forgive her that. No, the cutting part was that instead of flushing red or widening her eyes, like Daisy did, or even giving him a glimpse through her armour of tension and irritation like any other woman would have, Lucinda Myles had winced.

*Winced.* At the prospect of spending the night with him.

Daisy's eyes grew wider than ever and Ben decided it might be better for his reputation—and ego—if they moved this conversation elsewhere.

'Before you get entirely the wrong idea about my intentions,' he said, angling an arm behind Luce to guide her towards the bar, 'I should point out that I'm the owner of this hotel rather than an opportunistic guest. Ben Hampton, by the way.' A slow blink from Luce. Recognition? Ben pressed on anyway. 'And you should also know that the King James Suite has two very finely appointed bedrooms.'

Luce pursed her lips and eyed him speculatively before giving a sharp nod. 'Buy me a gin and tonic and you can explain exactly what you *did* mean by propositioning me in that manner while I try and find somewhere else to stay tonight.'

It wasn't entirely what he'd intended, but it would do. It would give her time to remember him, or for him to introduce himself all over again. And getting her even more tightly wound than usual would only make it more glorious when she fell apart under his touch.

# CHAPTER TWO

Luce smirked at Ben Hampton's retreating back and wondered what on earth had possessed the owner of a luxury hotel like the Royal Court to offer to share his suite with a complete stranger. Unless, of course, he remembered her, too. In which case, why hadn't he just said so? She was pretty sure Ben Hampton had never suffered from the sort of crippling embarrassment that sometimes held her back even now. He certainly hadn't when he was twenty.

Ben Hampton. Of course it was. She remembered that same scarred eyebrow raised at her over the breakfast table— a subtle mocking of the fact that while he and Mandy had been out having fun she'd been in studying. Again. They'd never been friends, never had any real meaningful conversations. Not even that last night, at another of his dad's swanky hotels for Ben's twenty-first birthday. She hadn't known him and she'd never cared to. The little she'd observed of him had told her his entire personality, and from what she'd seen today he hadn't changed. He still expected the world to bend to him and women to fall at his feet, just as he always had. And she still refused to do either. They were worlds apart— maybe even more so now than they had been at university.

So why offer her his room? For old times' sake?

Not that she'd be taking him up on the offer, of course. Especially if he didn't know who she was. Still, she had no reservations about acquiring a free drink from the exchange, while she worked on finding alternative accommodation.

Pulling out her phone again, Luce saw she had another message. Great. She dialled her voicemail and prepared to decipher her mother's rambling.

*'Lucinda? Are you there, darling? No? Are you sure?'*

A pause while Tabitha Myles waited to see if her eldest daughter was simply pretending to be an answering machine. Listening, Luce closed her eyes and shook her head a little.

*'Well, in that case, I suppose I should...maybe I should call back later? Except Tom did ask... You see, the thing is, darling, Tom's decided he should spend Christmas Day with his new girlfriend. Vanessa. Did he tell you about her? She sounds delightful. She has two children, I understand, and you know how Tom loves children... Anyway, since he won't be with us on Christmas Day we thought it might be nice to have a family dinner at the house on Christmas Eve so we can all meet Vanessa! Won't that be lovely? I think this could be a real step forward for him... after everything. And you always say the house still belongs to all of us, really. Dolly says she'll come too, as long as you're making your special chocolate puddings. I told her of course you would. And you can invite that lovely man of yours along. Been ages since we saw Dennis. Anyway, so that's that sorted. Friday evening, yes? See you then, darling. Lovely to talk to you. Bye!'*

Fantastic. It was Monday afternoon and she was stuck in Chester at the conference until Thursday morning, assuming she found somewhere to stay. What the hell was she supposed to cook that was worthy of Tom's tentative first steps out of depression and into the world of love *and* went with chocolate pots for Dolly? Maybe she could amend her supermarket order if she could get online. Which just left getting the house in a state Tabitha could tolerate, explaining once again that Dennis was not her boyfriend and writing her conference report. Not to mention the completed draft she'd promised her publisher of her first book. The university did like its lecturers to publish.

'Looks like I'll be working on the train,' she muttered to herself, tugging her organiser from her bag to start a new 'To Do' list. She saved Tabitha's message and her voicemail moved swiftly onto a harried conference organiser, apologising profusely for a 'slight confusion' with the hotel booking arrangements. Luce could hear the poor girl's boss yelling in the background.

Sighing, Luce deleted the message. So, still homeless. Maybe she should call it quits and head back to Cardiff. She'd already given her lecture. And, interesting as the rest of the conference looked, it wasn't worth going without a bed for. Except her ticket was non-refundable, and the walk-up price would be astronomical. But if it meant she could just go home it might be worth it.

Her phone buzzed in her hand and Luce automatically swept a finger across the screen to open the e-mail. The cheery informality of Dennis's words set her teeth on edge from the first line.

Dr Luce! Bet you're living it up in Chester. Don't forget my summary on tomorrow's lecture, will you? D.

See? Things could be worse. Dennis could have come to Chester with her. Fortunately he was far too important and busy to spend time away from the university. That was why he sent Luce instead. Of course now she had to attend a really dull lecture on his behalf and take notes, but that was a price worth paying for his absence.

Tossing her phone onto the table, Luce scanned the bar to see where Ben had got to with her drink. She needed to formulate a plan to get through the next week, and that would definitely be easier with an icy G&T in her hand. Except it didn't look as if she'd be getting it any time soon.

At the bar, Ben Hampton had his phone clamped to his ear and was smiling at the redhead in the short skirt who'd claimed the barstool next to him. Typical. What did she expect from a man who offered to share his suite with a woman he barely knew? As if she needed further evidence that he hadn't changed since university. His sort never did. Luce remembered well enough Mandy stomping into the flat at two in the morning, more than once, wailing about how she'd caught Ben out with another woman. Remembered the one time he'd ever shown any interest in *her* at all, when Mandy hadn't been looking. Did he? she wondered. He'd been pretty drunk.

Luce narrowed her eyes as she observed him. But then he turned, leaning against the bar behind him, and raised that scarred eyebrow at Luce instead of at the redhead. A shiver ran across her shoulders and she glanced away. She really didn't have time for the sort of distractions Ben's smile promised. She had responsibilities, after all. And she knew far, far better than to get involved with men like Ben Hampton. Whatever game he was playing.

*Take responsibility. Take control.* She had to remember that.

Without looking up again, Luce grabbed her organiser and started planning how to get through her week.

Ben ignored his brother's voice in his ear and studied Luce instead. She was staring at her diary, where it rested on her crossed legs, and brushed an escaped strand of hair out of her eyes. Her pen was poised over the paper, but she wasn't writing anything. She looked like a woman trying to save the world one 'To Do' list at a time. His initial impression had definitely been right, even if he hadn't seen her in nearly a decade. This was a woman who needed saving from herself.

*Not my responsibility, though,* he reminded himself. *Not my fix this time.*

'So, what do you think?' Sebastian asked down the phone. 'Is it worth saving?'

'Definitely,' Ben answered, before realising that Seb was talking about the Royal Court Hotel, not Lucinda Myles. 'I mean, yes—I think it's worth working with.' The Royal Court was a relatively new acquisition, and Ben's job for the week was to find out how it ticked and how to make it work the Hampton & Sons way. 'You stayed here, right? Before we bought it? I mean, you must have done.'

'Dad did,' Seb said, his voice suddenly darker. 'I have his report, but...'

It was hard to ask questions about the room service and the bathroom refits when the old man was six feet under, Ben supposed. 'Right—sure. And there were concerns?'

'Perhaps.' Seb sounded exactly as their father had, whenever *he* hadn't said something that mattered. Keeping information from his youngest son because he didn't trust him to step up and do his job. To take responsibility for making things right.

Ben had hoped Seb knew him better than their father had. Apparently not.

Perhaps that was just what happened when you spent your childhood in different boarding schools. With five years between them, Ben had always been too far behind to catch up with his talented older brother. He'd always wondered what life had been like for Seb before he came along.

'Fine. I'll type up a new evaluation tonight and get it

over to you. Okay?' It wouldn't take long—especially if he could get the original report e-mailed over from head office. But work responsibilities could wait until later. First he had plans. Like finding out just how strokeable *Dr* Lucinda Myles really was under those clothes. Because *of course* she'd gone on to get her PhD. The woman was born for academia.

'That'd be great,' Seb said.

He sounded tired, and Ben could imagine him sitting behind Dad's big oak desk, rubbing a hand over his forehead. Because now it wasn't years and schools keeping them apart, it was the burden of responsibility.

Working together, especially since their father had died, had enabled Ben to get to know his brother better than ever before. They were close, he supposed, in their way. Possibly because neither of them really had anyone else.

And Seb was his brother before he was his boss. He had to remember that.

A stab of guilt at the thought made Ben ask, 'Is there anything else you need me to do?'

The pause at the other end of the line suggested that there was, but whatever it was Seb obviously didn't trust him to do it. 'Nah, don't worry about it. Enjoy your week in Chester. Take in a Roman relic or something. Or—no, you were planning on heading off to your cottage, weren't you?'

'I thought I might,' Ben said cautiously. God, after the last twelve months all he wanted was to hole up in the middle of nowhere with a good bottle of whisky, some really great music and some old movies. 'But if you need me back in the office—'

'No. You haven't had a holiday in nearly a year.' *Since before Dad died,* went unspoken. 'You deserve a break.'

Not as much as Seb did. The idea of persuading his ultra-

responsible older brother to take time off was frankly
laughable, but apparently Ben wasn't nearly as essential
to the well-being of Hampton & Sons. Something he might
as well take advantage of, he supposed. 'Well, you know
where I am if you need me.'

'In bed with a hot blonde?' his brother joked, a hint of
the old, relaxed Seb coming out.

Relief seeped through Ben at the sound of it. 'Brunette,
hopefully.' Ben eyed Luce again. Still ignoring him. If she
remembered him at all she probably felt exactly the same
way about him as his father had—that he was still the same
man she'd known him to be at twenty, incapable of growing up. Well, maybe he'd have a chance tonight to show
her exactly what sort of man he'd grown into.

Seb's laugh lacked any real humour. 'Then I wish you
luck. I'm sure you'll have her begging you for more in no
time.'

'That's the plan.'

'And then you'll just have to figure out how to get rid of
her when she inevitably loses her head over you.'

Quite aside from the fact that Ben found it impossible
to imagine Lucinda Myles losing her head over anyone,
something in Seb's words rankled.

'Hey, be fair. I'm always honest with them. They know
exactly what to expect. No commitment, no strings, no
future, and—'

'No more than one night together in a row,' Seb finished for him. 'I know. But they always think they'll be
the one to change you.'

Ben shrugged, even though Seb couldn't see him. 'Not
my responsibility. I don't do long-term.'

'Just the short-term fix.' Seb chuckled. 'Well, if that's
all you want enjoy yourself. I'll see you back in London
on Friday.' He hung up.

Ben put his brother's mocking out of his head. As if Seb was any better, anyway. Ben couldn't remember the last time he'd even seen him with a date.

Life was all about priorities, their father had always said. And just because Ben had never shared David Hampton's priorities when he was alive, and didn't intend to start now, that didn't make the sentiment any less valid.

His priorities weren't love and marriage. And his priority for the night certainly wasn't Seb and the business. It was Luce Myles. Grabbing two gin and tonics from the bartender, Ben was pretty sure he knew exactly how to get under her skin.

Luce's 'To Do' list was stretching to several pages by the time Ben finally returned with their drinks.

'Queue at the bar?' she asked, raising her eyebrows as he placed the glasses on the table. A girl couldn't be expected to deal with so many demands on her without a drink.

'Phone call from the office,' he countered with an apologetic smile.

She supposed that running a hotel chain did require some level of responsibility, hard though it was to imagine from Ben Hampton. On the other hand, he had described it as the 'Hampton & Sons' chain, so maybe he was just the heir apparent, running errands for Daddy, and the phone call was about him maxing out his company credit card. That would explain a lot, actually.

He folded himself into the low bucket chair, his long legs stretched out in front of him, and Luce allowed herself to be distracted from how the man made a living. A more interesting question was how did he manage to look so comfortable, so relaxed, in a chair so clearly not designed for someone of his height or size? Luce couldn't manage it, and the chair might have been made for her.

'You look like you kept yourself occupied, anyway.' He motioned at her list, and she winced.

'Busy week. Time of the year.' She started to close the cover of her organiser, but Ben's hand slipped between the pages and pushed it open again.

'Let's see what's keeping Dr Lucinda Myles so busy.'

Tugging the diary towards him, he flashed her a grin that made her middle glow a little, against her better judge-ment. She didn't remember him being this damn attractive. His behaviour was unacceptably intrusive, an invasion of her privacy, and her 'To Do' list was absolutely none of his business. And yet she didn't stop him. All because he had a wickedly attractive smile. Clearly she was losing her edge.

*I need some time off.* The thought was a familiar one, but Luce knew from past experience that nothing would come of it. Yes, some time to recharge her batteries—hell, even some time to focus on her book—would be benefi-cial. But when on earth would she ever find the time to make it happen?

Ben flipped through the list and gave a low whistle. 'Conference, followed by what I imagine to be a long and tedious conference report, family dinner party on Christ-mas Eve, Christmas Day entertaining, house repairs, cat-sitting for your neighbour, university New Year's Eve event, student evaluations, your actual day job. When were you planning on sleeping?'

'I wasn't.' Luce took a long sip of her gin and tonic. 'Es-pecially since I still don't have a bed for the night.'

'I believe I offered you a solution to that particular prob-lem.' Ben slammed her organiser shut, but kept his hand on it. 'In fact, after seeing your "To Do" list, I have an even better proposition.'

'So you *are* propositioning me, then?' Luce said, trying to sound accusing rather than amused. Or aroused. This was unacceptable behaviour—especially from the owner of a hotel. And she was not the sort of woman who had one-night stands in hotels just to get a bed for the night. However attractive the man. But part of her couldn't help wondering if he'd be doing this if he didn't remember her. Or, perhaps more likely, he'd never be doing this at all if he knew who she really was. *Which is it?*

Ben just smiled a lazy, seductive grin. 'Were you ever really in any doubt? Now, do you want to hear this proposition or not?'

She shouldn't. But her curious nature was what had led her into academia, into history, in the first place. She wanted to know what had happened, when and why. She couldn't help but remember all those long, dull evenings staying in to study, until Ben and Mandy stumbled into the flat, ready to tell her everything she'd missed, their eyes pitying. She needed to know what it was Ben Hampton saw in her *now* to make him waste his time trying to seduce her. 'Go on, then.'

'Take the night off.'

Luce blinked. 'That's it?'

Folding his arms behind his head, Ben smirked. 'It's elegant in its simplicity.'

'It's not possible.' Luce reached for her organiser, shaking her head. 'I need to type up my notes from today, I need to talk to my brother about this dinner, and I need to—'

'You need to slow down.' Peeling her fingers from the cover of her diary, Ben picked it up and slipped it into the pocket of his jacket.

Luce lunged across the table to try to grab it, but she was too slow. 'I need that. You can't just—'

'Trust me, it's for the best.' Luce glared at him, and

he sighed. 'Okay—tell you what. You listen to the rest of my plan, and if you honestly don't think it sounds like a good idea I'll give you your stupid planner back and you can go wander the streets of Chester looking for a hotel. All right?'

Even Luce had to admit that her options were a little limited. 'All right. What's the plan?'

'A night off. With me. You put on your best party dress, let me take you out to dinner. You talk about yourself—not the things you're supposed to be doing. You let me take responsibility for showing you a good time. You relax. We have a nightcap in my suite, and then you get a good night's sleep.'

'In my own room?' Luce stamped down on the corner of her mind that was happily imagining what might happen if they were both in *his* room.

Ben's smile grew a little wolfish. 'Well, now...that's up to you.'

'Really?' Luce said flatly.

'Of course.' Ben looked mildly offended. 'I'm not saying I won't give it my best shot. You're a beautiful woman, and I enjoy the company of beautiful women. But at the end of the night *you* get the choice of my bed or the spare room. Either way you have a bed for the night.'

Luce found her gaze caught on his. He thought she was beautiful? Ben Hampton actually wanted her? Sober, all grown-up, not obviously crazy...and he wanted her. She could have dinner with him, flirt, kiss...more. All she had to do was say yes.

She tore her gaze away.

'And tomorrow?' she asked.

Ben's smile slipped. 'Tomorrow I'm leaving town. Look, whichever way tonight goes, it's nothing sordid. Nothing to be ashamed of. We can enjoy each other's company then

go our separate ways. I'm not asking you for anything beyond tonight.'

'So romantic,' Luce muttered. She hated how unworldly
he made her feel. His matter-of-fact proposition of a one-
night stand was miles away from any date she'd been on
in the last ten years. And also the reason she couldn't give
in to it. She wanted more from a night of passion than a
kiss on the cheek at the end of it and never seeing each
other again.

'This isn't romance,' Ben said. 'It's much more fun than
that. And, either way, I bet you feel better in the morning.'

And she would. Sex aside, she'd get a stress-free evening, with no need to entertain since Ben was clearly capable of making his own fun. She could just relax and let
someone else take charge for a few hours. Could she even
*do* that? She wasn't sure she ever had before.

'Admit it—you're tempted.'

Ben leant across the table, that scarred eyebrow raised,
and Luce knew that she was. In more ways than one.

'By dinner,' she told him firmly. 'Nothing else.'

Ben gave her a lazy smile. 'As you like.'

It might be the worst idea she'd ever had. But at least
she'd have somewhere to sleep for the night, and the whole
week ahead would look more manageable after a relaxing
evening and a solid eight hours' rest. And maybe tomorrow morning she could tell him who she was and watch
his amused composure slip as he realised he'd tried to
seduce Loser Luce. Again. That would almost make it
worth it in itself.

*I shouldn't. I have responsibilities.*

But even Grandad Myles, duty and responsibility's big-
gest advocate, would have wanted her to take a night off
once in a while. Wouldn't he? She was stressed, over-
whelmed and exhausted—and utterly useless to anybody

in such a state. A night off to regroup would enable her to better help others and get things done more efficiently. Nothing at all to do with wanting to find out what she'd been missing on all those university nights out.

Besides, hadn't she fantasised about a night in the Royal Court's best suite?

'On one condition,' she said.

Ben grinned. 'Anything.'

'I want to take advantage of your hopefully plush and expensive bathroom first.' With bubbles. And maybe champagne.

Ben's grin grew wider. 'Deal.'

'Then give me my organiser back.' She was already starting to feel a bit jittery without it. Maybe she could review her lists in the bath. Multi-tasking—that was the key to a productive life.

But Ben shook his head. 'First thing tomorrow it's all yours. Not one moment before.'

'But I need—'

'Trust me,' Ben said, taking her hand in his across the table. 'Tonight I'll be in charge of meeting all your needs.'

A red-hot flush ran across Luce's skin. Perhaps this wasn't such a good idea after all.

# CHAPTER THREE

Luce had never seen such a magnificent bathroom.

The size of the rolltop tub almost helped her forget the sight of Ben locking her beloved crimson leather organiser in the suite's mini-safe. And the glass of champagne he'd poured her before she'd absconded to the bathroom more than made up for the way she'd blushed when he'd asked if she was sure she didn't want him to help scrub her back.

Tearing her eyes away from the bath, Luce checked the door, then turned the lock. She'd told him as clearly as she could that the only part of his offer she was interested in was dinner and the spare bed. No point giving him the wrong idea now.

Of course she wasn't entirely sure what the right idea was. Accepting an offer of a night out with a gorgeous man—whatever the terms and conditions—wasn't exactly typical Luce behaviour. She hadn't even made a pros and cons list, for a start.

But the decision was made now. She might as well make the most of it.

Turning on the taps, Luce rifled through the tiny bottles of complimentary lotions and potions, settling on something that claimed to be a 'relaxing and soothing' bath foam. Sounded perfect. After a moment's consideration she tipped the whole bottle into the running water. She

was in need of all the relaxation she could get. That was
the point of this whole night, wasn't it? And, since it was
the only one she was likely to get for a while, she really
should make the most of it.

Luce took a swig of her champagne, stripped off her
clothes and climbed into the heavenly scented hot water.

Relaxation. How hard could it be?

It would be a whole lot easier, she decided after a few
moments of remaining tense, if Ben Hampton wasn't waiting outside for her.

Tipping her head back against the edge of the bath,
Luce tried to conjure up the image of the last time she'd
seen him. After so many years of trying to forget she'd
thought it would be harder to remember. But the sounds,
scents, sights were all as fresh in her mind as they'd been
eight years ago, at the swanky Palace Hotel, London, for
Ben's twenty-first birthday party.

It had been a stupid idea to go in the first place. But
Mandy had wanted someone to travel down on the train
with and Ben had raised his eyebrows in surprise and said,
'Well, sure you can come. If you really want to.' And Luce
*had* wanted to—just a bit. Just to see what birthdays looked
like for the rich and privileged.

Much as she'd expected, it turned out. Too much champagne. Too many people laughing too loudly. Bright lights
and dancing and shimmery expensive dresses. In her green
cotton frock, and with her hair long and loose instead of
pinned back in one of the intricate styles the other girls
had seemed to favour, Luce had felt just as out of place as
she'd predicted.

So she'd hidden in another room—some sort of sitting
area decked out like a gentleman's library. Books never
made her feel inadequate, after all. She could sit and read
until Mandy was ready to head back to their tiny shared

hotel room. Not a Hampton hotel, but a cheap, probably infested place three tube stops away. It had been the perfect plan—until Ben had found her.

'You've got the right idea,' he'd said, lurching into the chair next to her.

Luce, who'd already watched him down glass after glass of champagne that evening, had inched further away. 'Not enjoying your party?' she'd asked.

Ben had shrugged. 'It's a party. Hard not to enjoy a party.' His eyes had narrowed as he'd studied her. 'Although you seem to be managing it.'

Looking away, Luce had fiddled with the hem of her dress. 'It's not really my kind of party.'

'It's not really mine either,' Ben had said.

When Luce had glanced across at him he'd been staring at the door. But then his attention had jerked back to her, and a wide, not entirely believable grin had been on his face. 'It's just my dad showing off, really. There are more of his business associates here than my friends.'

'And yet you invited me?'

He'd laughed at that. 'We're friends, aren't we?'

'Not really.' They'd had nothing in common besides proximity to Mandy until that moment, right then, when Luce had felt his gaze meeting hers, connecting them— until she'd realised she was leaning forward, into him, waiting for his answer.

'We could be.'

He'd inched closer too, leaning over the arm of his chair until Luce had been able to smell the champagne on his breath.

'You're a hell of a lot of a nicer person than Mandy.'

'Mandy's my friend,' Luce had said, trying to find the energy to defend her. But all she'd been able to see was

Ben's eyes, pupils black and wide. 'Your girlfriend.' She couldn't think with him so close.

'Mandy's out there flirting with a forty-something businessman she knows will never leave his wife but might buy her some nice jewellery.'

Luce had winced. He was probably right. For a moment she'd felt her first ever pang of sympathy for Ben Hampton.

But then he'd leant in further, his hand coming up to rest against her cheek, and Luce had known she should pull away, run away, get away from Ben Hampton for good.

His lips had been soft, gentle against hers, she remembered. But only for a brief moment. One insane lapse in judgement. Before she jerked back, leaving him bent over the space where she'd been. She'd upped and run—just as she should have done the moment she'd arrived at the party and seen how much she didn't fit in.

Luce sighed and let the memory go. Much more pleasant to focus on the hot water and scented bubbles of her bath than on Ben's face as she'd turned back at the doorway. Or the humiliation she'd felt, her cheeks burning, as she'd run out, his laughter echoing in her ears, and dragged Mandy away from her businessman and back to that flea-ridden hotel.

He probably didn't remember. He'd been drunk and young and stupid. He'd certainly never have done it sober. Why else would he have laughed? The whole incident was ridiculous. Luce was a grown woman now, with bigger concerns than what Ben Hampton thought of her.

Except he was waiting outside the bathroom door, ready to take her out for dinner. And afterwards...

Luce shut her eyes and dunked her head under the water.

What the hell was she doing in there?

Ben checked his watch, then poured himself another

glass of champagne. It was coming up to three quarters of an hour since he'd heard the lock turn, and since then there had been only the occasional splash. Apparently she was taking the whole relaxing thing seriously. He should have remembered earlier how his ex-girlfriend had complained about Luce disappearing into the bathroom with her history texts and using up all the hot water on ridiculously indulgent baths. At the time he'd just found it comforting to know that the woman had some weaknesses. Now it was seriously holding up his evening.

But at least it gave him the opportunity to do some research. Unlocking the safe, he pulled out Luce's organiser again and sank into the armchair by the window to read. Really, the woman was the epitome of over-scheduled. And almost none of the things written into the tiny diary spaces in neat block capitals seemed like things she'd be doing for herself. Christmas dinners—plural—for family, attending lectures for colleagues, looking after someone else's cat... And then, on a Sunday near the end of January, the words 'BOOK DRAFT DEADLINE' in red capitals. Interesting. Definitely something to talk about over dinner.

She baffled him. That was why he wanted to know more. On the one hand, he was pretty sure he could predict her entire life story leading from university to here. On the other, however...there was something else there. Something he hadn't seen or noticed when they were younger. Something that hooked him in even if he wasn't ready to admit why. Yes, she was attractive. That on its own was nothing new. But this self-sacrificing mentality—was it a martyr complex? A bullying mother? Luce hadn't ever seemed weak, so why was she doing everything for other people?

Particularly her family, it seemed. Flicking through the pages, Ben tried to remember if he'd ever met them at university, but if he had they hadn't made much of an impression. Now he thought about it, he did remember Luce disappearing home to Cardiff every few weeks to visit them.

Obviously a sign of things to come.

Leaning back in his chair, Ben closed the organiser and tried to resist the memories pressing against his brain. But they were too strong. Another dark-haired woman, just as tired, just as self-sacrificing—until the day she broke.

*'I'm sorry, Benji,'* she'd said. *'Mummy has to go.'*

And it didn't matter that he'd tried everything, done anything he could think of to be good enough to make her stay. He hadn't been able to fix things for her.

Maybe he could for Luce.

Laughing at himself, he sat up, shaking the memories away. Luce wasn't his mother. She wasn't tied by marriage or children. She could make her own choices far more freely. And what could he do in one night, anyway? Other than help her relax. Maybe that would be enough. Maybe all she needed was to realise that she had needs, too. And Ben was very good at assessing women's needs.

A repetitive beeping noise interrupted his thoughts, and it took him a moment to register it as a ringtone. As he looked up, his gaze caught on Luce's rich purple coat, slung across the sofa on the other side of the glass coffee table. She'd taken her suitcase and handbag into the bathroom with her—obvious paranoia in Ben's view—but he'd seen her drop her phone into her coat pocket before they left the bar.

Interesting.

He should feel guilty, he supposed, but really it was all for the woman's own good. She needed saving from herself. She needed his help.

The noise had stopped before he could retrieve the

phone from the pocket of her coat, and Ben stared at the flashing screen for a moment, wondering how one woman could have so many people needing to contact her. In addition to a missed call from her mother, her notifications screen told him straight off that she had three texts from a guy called Tom, an e-mail from a man named Dennis and another missed call from an improbably named 'Dolly'. All in the hour since they'd left the bar.

Scanning over the snippets on the screen told him all he really needed to know—every person who'd contacted her wanted something from her. Dropping the phone back into her pocket, Ben considered the evening ahead.

His plan, ill thought out to start with, had been to have a fun evening and hopefully a fun night. To show Luce a good time, then remind her who he was so they could have a laugh about it. Or *he* could, anyway. But now...he was invested.

Who *was* Lucinda Myles these days?

The last time he'd seen her must have been the night of his spectacularly disastrous twenty-first birthday party. He remembered spotting her sloping out of the hotel ballroom towards one of the drawing rooms, but after that far too much champagne had blurred the evening until the following morning and a headbangingly loud lecture from his father about appropriate behaviour and responsibility to the family reputation. Friends had helpfully filled him in on the more humorous of his antics that night, but no one had mentioned Luce.

Then the ex had broken up with him for humiliating her and 'possibly ruining her future', whatever that meant, and he'd had no reason to see Luce again. Who knew how much she'd changed in the intervening years?

Ben paused in his thoughts. She couldn't have changed

that much, given what he'd seen so far that day. In which case...

Grabbing the phone from the table next to him, he called down to Reception.

'Daisy? Can you cancel my booking at The Edge to-night?' Trendy, stainless-steel, cutting-edge fusion restaurants just weren't Luce's style, no matter who the concierge had needed to bribe to get him a table there that night. 'No, don't worry. I'll sort out an alternative myself.'

Something more Luce. More fun too, probably.

One more quick phone call ascertained that the restaurant he was thinking of still existed. Perfect. Hanging up, Ben glanced at the bathroom door and then at his watch again. He'd given Luce long enough. Time to move on to the next stage of their evening.

Pausing first to replace the diary in the safe, he gave the bathroom door a quick rap with his knuckles and then said, loud enough to be sure he could be heard through it, 'You've got five more minutes in there before I start trying to guess the pass code for your phone.'

To his surprise, the lock turned and the door opened almost instantly. Eyebrows raised, Luce stared at him and said, 'Threats aren't traditionally very relaxing, you know.'

But baths clearly were. Especially for Dr Lucinda Myles.

She'd changed out of those clothes he'd been longing to run his hands over, but since she'd replaced them with a slippery, silky purple dress he really wasn't complaining. Her hair was pinned up off her neck, with a few damp tendrils curling behind her ears and across her forehead. She smiled at him, her deep red lips curving in amusement. 'I didn't think you were the sort of man to do speechless. I like it.'

A rush of lavender hit his lungs as she swept past him,

reminding him of the château in summer, and he realised he still hadn't spoken. 'If I'd known you were using your time so well I'd have been much more patient,' he said, finding his voice at last.

Luce slipped her arms into her coat, her fingers reaching into the pocket for her phone. Time for another distraction. Ben offered her his arm and she took it, forestalling her return to the world of technology and messages from people who wanted far less fun things from her than he did. 'Now, if you're ready, won't you let me escort you to dinner?'

She still looked suspicious as she nodded, but she left the room beside him, steady on higher heels than he'd have expected her to be comfortable wearing. Ben smiled. This was going to be a good evening. He was sure of it. The hotel and the business were fine, and he had the company of a beautiful and intriguing woman for the night—one he might be able to help a little. And then he'd get to decamp to the cottage for the rest of the week, feeling good about himself.

Life was great.


There should be laws against men looking quite that good in a suit. Men she was determined to resist, anyway. If Dennis had ever looked even half as good maybe they would have managed more than a few coffees and the occasional fake date when he needed a partner for a university dinner or she needed someone for a family event.

Actually, no, they wouldn't. Quite aside from the fact that Dennis became intensely irritating after more than a couple of hours in his company, she'd never felt that... *spark*—that connection she needed to take the risk of building an actual relationship. To her surprise, Ben Hampton had a spark. Not a relationship one, of course, but maybe something more intense. Something that definitely hadn't been there the last time they met. Which was just as well, as he'd been dating her roommate at the time. But there was definitely something.

It was almost a shame she didn't have the time, energy or courage to take him up on his offer to find out exactly what.

Her phone buzzed in her pocket and her fingers itched to reach for it. She hadn't called her mother back, and she'd only worry if she didn't hear from her. Well, actually, she probably wouldn't. Tabitha saved her concern for Tom and Dolly, safe in the knowledge that Luce could take care of herself far better than the rest of them.

Still, she'd get annoyed, which was even worse, and pull a guilt trip on Luce next time they spoke.

She really should call her back. But Ben's arm held her hand trapped against his body, and she could feel the warmth of him even through his coat and suit jacket. Was that intentional? Trying to cut her off from her real life and keep her in this surreal bubble of a night he'd created?

Ben Hampton had invaded her life and her personal space since she'd bumped into him again, only a couple of hours ago, and she'd let him. Sat back and let him take charge, point out the problems in her life, rearrange all her plans for the evening. What had happened to taking responsibility and control?

Okay, she needed a new plan for the night. Something to wrest back control. At the very least she needed to know if he remembered her...

She shivered as they left the hotel lobby, the bitter night air stinging her face and her lungs. Icicle Christmas lights dangled above the cobbled streets, twinkling in the night like the real thing. Ben tugged her a little closer, and she wondered how it was he stayed so warm despite the winter chill.

'Where are we going?' she asked, belatedly realising he hadn't even told her where he was taking her. Some fancy restaurant, probably, she'd figured when pulling out the dress she'd packed for the conference gala dinner. But that wasn't the point. No one knew where she was—least of all her. It was madness. She was out in a strange city at night with a man she barely knew. A little surreptitious internet searching in the bar while he'd been fetching the drinks had told her the bare bones of his professional career since university—which mostly seemed to be doing whatever his father needed him to do—but it hadn't told her what sort of a man he was. She hadn't seen him in eight years, and she hadn't known him all that well back then. He certainly hadn't been the kind of guy the twenty-year-old Luce had willingly spent time with. This was foolishness beyond compare. Dennis would be horrified.

Of course her mother would probably be relieved. Tabitha had always been a little afraid that her daughter had inherited none of her more flighty attributes at all.

'A little French restaurant I know,' Ben said, answering the question she'd almost forgotten she'd asked. 'It's up past the Cross, on the Rows. You okay to walk in those shoes?'

'Of course.' Luce spoke the words automatically, even though the balls of her feet had started to smart as she struggled over the cobbles. *Show no weakness.* That was another of her grandad's rules to live by. If she couldn't keep the other one tonight, she might as well try to hang on to something.

'You never used to wear shoes like that.'

Luce couldn't tell if the warm feeling that settled over her shoulders at Ben's words was relief or confusion. 'You do remember me, then?' she blurted out before she could stop herself. 'I wasn't sure.'

'You think I invite strange women up to my suite all the time?'

Luce shrugged. 'University was a long time ago. I have no idea what kind of man you are now. And, actually...'

'Yeah, yeah.' Ben rolled his eyes. 'Eight years ago I'd have invited *all* women up to my room.'

'I hope you've grown up a little since then.' A hitch in Ben's step made her glance up. 'What?'

He shook his head. 'Nothing. Just depends who you ask.'

Picking up speed again, Ben led them up the very steep steps onto the medieval Rows, a second layer of shops and restaurants above the street-level ones. The historian in Luce was fascinated by the structure—the timber fronts, the overhanging storey above making a covered walkway. There was no other example in the world—the Chester Rows were unique. She should be savouring every detail.

And instead all she could think was, *He remembers me.* Well, at least she knew now. Except...just because he remembered her, that didn't mean he remembered the last time they'd seen each other.

Maybe he'd forgotten it entirely. And maybe that meant she could, too.

It was too cold for much more conversation. They made their way along the Rows, Luce tucked tightly into Ben's body for warmth, until he said, 'Here we are,' and Luce's whole body relaxed at the sight of a cosy little restaurant tucked away behind a few closed shops with sparkling Christmas window displays.

'Thank God for that,' she said, smiling up at Ben. 'I'm freezing.'

# CHAPTER FOUR

SMILING UP AT HIM, complaining about the cold, Luce seemed relaxed for the first time. As if this was any usual date, not a peculiar arrangement to help an uptight woman cut loose. And she remembered him. That was a start. He wasn't sure he could have made it all through dinner without knowing.

Ben pushed open the door to La Cuillère d'Argent and let Luce walk into the warmth first. Her face brightened in the candlelit restaurant, and she glanced back at him with surprise on her face.

'I'm overdressed,' she said, taking in the rustic wooden tables and chairs. There weren't many other people eating there, but those who were wore mostly casual clothes.

'You look perfect.' He smiled at the waiter approaching. 'Table for two, please?'

Seated at a candlelit table in the window, looking out at the people hurrying past, Luce stripped off her coat and asked, 'How did you know about this place?'

'Not what you were expecting?'

She shook her head, and Ben knew what she was thinking. She'd expected somewhere impressive, somewhere fancy and expensive—somewhere that would make her feel kindly towards him when he paid, possibly impressed enough to take him to bed when they got back to the hotel.

Somewhere like The Edge. Somewhere that said, *I'm Ben Hampton and I've just inherited half of a multi-million-pound hotel chain, and I still have time to flatter and treat you. Aren't you impressed?*

But that would have defeated the object of the evening. He wanted Luce to relax, and he knew she wasn't the sort to be impressed by or enjoy over-priced, over-fiddly food. Too practical for that, with her epic 'To Do' lists and her martyr complex. She'd probably feel guilty the whole time, which wouldn't help his cause at all.

No, he needed somewhere cosy and intimate, somewhere he could actually talk to her, learn about her life since uni, find out what made her tick. This place was perfect for that. Ben blinked in the candlelight as he realised, belatedly, that he *wanted* to know her. Not just seduce her or entertain her. He wanted to know the truth of Luce Myles.

Of course seducing her was still firmly part of the plan. He just didn't mind a little small talk first.

'Have you been here before?' Luce asked, scanning the wine list. 'Do you live in Chester?'

Ben shook his head. 'Just visiting to check on the hotel. But I came here with my mother years ago. She was born in France, you see. Knew every great French restaurant in the country.' It must have been fifteen years ago or more, he realised. 'I checked while you were in the bath to make sure it was still here, actually. It really has been a while.'

'What does it mean?' Luce asked, staring at the front of the menu, where the restaurant name curled across the card. '"La Cuillère d'Argent",' she read slowly.

'The Silver Spoon,' Ben translated, tapping a finger against the picture under the words—an ornate piece of silverware not unlike the ones on the table for their use.

'I like it,' Luce announced, smiling at him over the menu.

Ben's shoulders dropped as a tension he hadn't realised he was feeling left him. That was wrong. She was the one who was supposed to be relaxing. He was always relaxed. That was who he was.

'Good,' he said, a little unnerved, and motioned a waiter over to order a carafe of white wine to start. He rather thought he might need it tonight.

They made polite conversation about the menu options, and the freshly baked bread with olive tapenade the waiter brought them, before Luce asked, 'So, if you're just visiting, where is home these days?'

Ben shrugged. Home wasn't exactly something he associated with his stark and minimalist penthouse suite. And since he hadn't been to the cottage in Wales for over a year, and the château in France for far longer, he was pretty sure they didn't count.

'I'm based out of London, but mostly I'm on the road. Wherever there's a Hampton & Sons hotel I've got a bed for the night, so I do okay.'

Across the table Luce's eyes widened with what Ben recognised as pity. 'That must be hard. Not having anywhere to call home.'

Must it? 'I'm used to it, I guess. Even growing up, I lived in the hotels.' A different one every time he came home from boarding school, after his mother left. 'I've got a penthouse suite in one of the London hotels to crash in, if I want. Fully serviced and maintained.'

'Thus neatly getting out of one of the joys of home ownership,' Luce said wryly.

Ben remembered the 'House Repairs' entry on her 'To Do' list.

'Your house takes some upkeep, then?'

'It's falling apart,' Luce said, her voice blunt, and reached for her wine. 'But it was my grandfather's house, and I grew up there. I could never sell it even if I found someone willing to take it on.'

'Still, sounds like a lot of work on top of all your other commitments.' Was this something else she was doing for her family? For the sake of others? 'Are you sure you wouldn't be happier in a cosy little flat near the university?'

He was mostly joking, so the force of her reply surprised him. *'Never.'*

'Okay.'

Dropping her eyes to the table, Luce shook her head a little before smiling up at him. 'Sorry. It's just…I worry about it a lot. But one day I'll finish fixing the place up and it'll be the perfect family home. It's just getting there that's proving trying.'

Ben shrugged. 'I guess I don't really get it. I mean, I own properties and such. I've even renovated one of them. But they're just bricks and mortar to me. If I had to sell them, or if getting rid of them gave me another opportunity— well, it wouldn't worry me.'

'You don't get attached, huh?' She gave him a lopsided smile. 'Probably a good choice if you're always moving around.'

'Exactly. Don't get tied down. It's one of my rules for life.'

'Yeah? What are the others?'

Ben couldn't tell if she was honestly interested or mocking him. 'Most importantly: enjoy life. And avoid responsibility, of course.'

'Of course,' she echoed with a smile, reaching for the bread basket. 'You never were big on that.'

There was an awkward silence while Ben imagined Luce rerunning every stupid moment he'd had at university in her head. Time to change the subject.

'So, you're in Chester for some conference thing?' he asked.

Luce nodded, swallowing the bread she was chewing. '*"Bringing History to the Future".*' Ben smiled at the sarcasm in her voice.

'You're not a fan?'

'It's not that,' Luce replied with a shrug. 'It's just… there's so much important preservation and research to be done, and finding a way to make the importance of our history fit into a series of thirty-minute television programmes with accompanying books does tend to interfere a bit.'

'But if it's not important to the bulk of the populace…?'

'Then we lose funding and the chance to study important sites and documents. I know, I know…'

From the way she waved her hands in a dismissive manner Ben gathered this wasn't the first time she'd heard the argument. 'You have this debate a lot?'

Luce gave him a lopsided smile. 'Mostly with myself. I understand the need, but sometimes I'd rather be holed up in a secluded library somewhere, doing real research, real work, not worrying about who was going to read and dissect it without understanding the background.'

'This is your book?' Ben tore himself another piece of bread and smeared it with tapenade, but kept his gaze on her.

Luce pulled a face. 'My book is somewhere between the two. "Popular history for armchair historians," my editor calls it. Or it will be if I ever finish it.'

'What's it about?'

'An obscure Welsh princess who became the mistress of Henry I, and whose rape caused the end of the truce between the Normans and the Welsh.' The words sounded rote, as if she'd been telling people the same line for a long time without making any progress.

Ben scoured his vague memory of 'A' Level history, but they hadn't covered much Welsh history in his very English boarding schools. 'You're still based in Wales, then?' he asked.

Luce nodded. 'Cardiff. But not just for the history. It's where I grew up. Where my family lives. It's home. And when Grandad left me the house I knew it was where I was meant to stay.'

'That's nice,' Ben said absently, thinking again of the overgrown château that was his heritage from his maternal grandmother. He should probably check in on it some time soon.

The waiter brought their meals, and the conversation moved on to discussing the dishes in front of them.

'So,' he said, when they'd both agreed their food was delicious, and Luce had stolen a bite of his rabbit with mustard sauce, 'tell me more about this Welsh princess of yours.'

Her eyebrows jumped up in surprise. 'You're interested?'

'I have a cottage in Wales,' he explained. 'Down in the Brecons. It's where I'm headed tomorrow, actually. A good story might get me in the right mood for my rural retreat.'

'What do you want to know?'

Ben shrugged. 'Everything.'

The surprised look stayed, but Luce obliged all the same.

'Um…Princess Nest. She was the daughter of the King of Deheubarth, in South West Wales, and she gave Henry I a son before he married her off to his steward in Wales.'

'Nice of him,' Ben murmured.

'How things worked then. Anyway, the reason she's remembered, really, is her abduction.'

'She was kidnapped?' Letting his fork drop to his plate, Ben started paying real attention. Against the odds, this was actually interesting.

Luce nodded. 'Owain ap Cadwgan, the head of the Welsh resistance, fell in love with her. He and his men stole into Cilgerran Castle and took her.'

Ben blinked. 'What happened next?'

'A lot of things.' Luce smiled. 'A whole book's worth, in fact. Some people say she fell in love with Owain, too. But really, if you want to know the whole story, you'll have to read my book.'

'I will,' Ben promised. If she ever finished writing it, of course.

Okay, she had to give Ben Hampton this much—he was a better judge of restaurants than she'd expected. And a better conversationalist than she remembered. He'd actually sounded interested when she'd talked about Princess Nest and her book, which was more than anyone in her family had ever managed. Of course he was only doing it to get her into bed—she wasn't stupid, and he'd all but told her as much—but she had no qualms at all about turning him down at the bedroom door. She couldn't imagine for a moment that someone with the charm and self-confidence of Ben Hampton would have any trouble shaking off that kind of rejection.

She, on the other hand, had absolutely no desire to be the one being ushered out of the bedroom before breakfast the next morning, when he'd got what he wanted and lost interest in her.

The waiter cleared away their dessert plates and deposited the coffees they'd ordered in front of them, along with two oversized liqueur glasses with a small amount of thick amber liquid pooled at the base.

'Calvados,' Ben explained, lifting his glass to his lips. 'Apple brandy. It's a traditional Normandy *digestif.*'

Luce followed suit. The brandy taste she remembered from occasional late nights with her grandfather during university holidays was deepened by the hint of fruit. 'It's good.'

Ben shrugged. 'I like it.'

While she was drinking it he paid the bill. She realised too late to insist on paying her half. 'Let me give you something for my—'

'Absolutely not.'

Ben clamped a hand down over hers as she reached for her purse, and she felt the thrill of a shiver running up her wrist to her shoulder. It must be the brandy, she decided, affecting her judgement. Because, however attractive Ben Hampton was, and however intense his focus on her and her conversation made her feel, she was not going to sleep with him tonight.

She couldn't help but wonder, though, how all that concentration on the moment would feel if he was focusing it on her body. Her pleasure.

Luce shook her head. Too much Calvados. Some fresh air would sort that out.

Ben slipped her coat over her shoulders, and that same frisson ran through her as he stood close behind her. Luce wondered whether her room in the suite had a lock on its door. For keeping him out or her in, she wasn't entirely sure.

The cold night air bit into the exposed skin of her face and hands. Luce glanced at her watch: nearly midnight. She needed to get some sleep if she was going to make that lecture for Dennis in the morning. She huddled into her coat and felt Ben's arm settle on her shoulders, holding her close against him again.

'So, feeling any more relaxed?' he asked.

'Lots,' Luce answered honestly. 'But that might just be the alcohol.'

'True.'

They walked a few more steps, and Luce almost thought he might drop the subject.

Then he asked, 'So, what do you think might relax you a little more?'

*Truly great sex,* Luce thought, but didn't say. The sort that made you forget your own name, just for a little while. The sort that let you sleep so deeply you woke refreshed and energised, however much of the night you'd spent exploring each other's bodies.

Not that she'd ever actually *had* sex like that herself, of course. But Dolly was adamant that it existed.

'Um…handing in my book draft on time?' she said finally, when she realised he was still waiting for an answer.

'And how do you plan to do that when your "To Do" list is full of stuff you need to do for other people?'

It was a question she'd asked herself often enough, but hearing it in Ben's relaxed, carefree voice made her bristle. 'What do you care? If you're so against helping others, why do you care if I get my book in or not?'

Ben shrugged. 'Well, I've listened to Nest's life story this evening. I'm invested now. I told you—I want to read the damn thing when you finish it.'

'Oh.' Luce tried to hide her astonishment.

'Besides, I didn't say I was against helping others. I'm here in Chester because I'm doing a favour for my brother.'

Apparently he wasn't going to stop surprising her any time soon.

'What favour?'

'The person who was supposed to be checking out the hotel this week got sick, so I offered to swing by on my way to a week off.'

Ben smiled down at her, and Luce felt it in her cold bones.

'So, you see, it's not helping out others I object to.'

'Then what is it?' Luce asked, remembering that she was supposed to be annoyed.

'I object to you giving up your whole life to serve others. I think you need to put your own wants and needs first for a while.'

It sounded so reasonable when he said it. So tempting. But then Luce remembered the pages of 'To Do' lists filling her stolen organiser. 'And how, exactly, do you suggest I do that?'

'Well, actually,' Ben said, grinning, 'I do have one idea.'

They were nearly back at the hotel now. Luce stopped walking and raised her eyebrows. 'Are you really trying to tell me that sleeping with you would solve all my problems?'

Ben chuckled. 'No. But it would be a good start.'

Luce closed her eyes and laughed. 'You are incorrigible.'

'Come on,' he said, tugging her forward again. 'Let's get inside.'

# CHAPTER FIVE

THE SUITE WAS almost too hot after the bite of the December night air. Ben stripped off his coat and jacket, rolling up his shirtsleeves as he made his way across to the bar area. 'What can I get you? More brandy?'

'Um…peppermint tea?' Luce asked.

He couldn't help but smile at her. 'Is that to help you resist my charms?' he asked.

'To help me get up for this lecture in the morning.'

Luce sprawled into the chair he'd been sitting in earlier, and Ben admired the way her slim calves stretched out in front of her. She'd kicked her shoes off the moment they'd got into the room, and she pointed her toes as she flexed her feet.

There was absolutely no reason at all for that to be sexy. And yet…

Flicking on the kettle, he said, 'I wanted to talk to you about that, actually.' If she wasn't going to let him help her relax the way he knew best, maybe he could at least draw her attention to some of the unnecessary things that were stressing her out.

Luce raised her eyebrows at him and waited for him to continue.

'What is it, exactly, that you'll get out of attending this lecture for a colleague?'

'It's a favour,' Luce said. 'I'm not expecting to get anything out of it.'

'So this guy won't do the same for you at a later date? It's not somehow tangentially related to your own research and might prove helpful one day? The university won't look fondly on your actions and bear it in mind in the future when it comes to promotions and such?' He was watching carefully, so he saw her squirm a little in her seat. Had she never considered how little she got back from all she gave out?

'Well, no. Not really.' She shifted again, looking down at her hands. 'Dennis doesn't like leaving the university much, and I can't imagine he'll let on to anyone at the university that I went for him in the first place. Plus the topic's pretty dull.'

The kettle boiled and Ben poured hot water onto a tea bag in one of the fine china mugs. Then he poured himself a large brandy while it brewed. 'In that case, I can only assume that this man is important to you in some way. Are you dating?'

'No!'

The answer was so quick and so vehement that Ben suspected he wasn't the first person to suspect it. But maybe it wouldn't bother her so much if it wasn't him asking. He could hope, anyway.

'Then why are you doing it?'

'Because he asked,' Luce said, sounding miserable.

'And you can't say no?'

Her glare was scathing. 'I said no to you, didn't I?'

Ben took her the tea before he replied. 'You told me you wouldn't stay here tonight, and now you are.'

'I told you I wouldn't sleep with you. I'm holding firm on that one.'

He chuckled, and saw her frown grow deeper. Had she

always been this much fun to tease? How had he not noticed? 'We'll see. Anyway, the point is you do all these
things for other people and you get nothing back. You need
to think about what you want for yourself.'

Luce sighed into her cup of tea. 'I know.'

She sounded defeated, which wasn't quite what Ben had
been going for. She hadn't stopped fighting him since they
met in the lobby. He kind of liked that about her.

'But there's just never any time. If I don't take care of
things for Tom, or Dolly, or Mum, it'll just cause a bigger mess further along the line that I'll have to clear up.'

'Tom and Dolly—your brother and sister?' He didn't
remember her even talking about her family at university.
Not that they'd ever really had any long, meaningful talks
about their lives, of course. But he was starting to wish
they had. Maybe then Luce would make more sense to him.

Luce nodded. 'They…they're not very good at getting
by on their own. Neither is Mum. It was different when
Grandad was still alive. But now…'

'They all rely on you.' Ben slouched down in his chair,
stretching his foot out to nudge against hers. 'Sounds to
me like you need someone you can rely on for a change.'

Her head jerked up in surprise. 'You cannot possibly
be suggesting that person is you.'

'Good God, no!' Ben shuddered at the very thought.
'Good for one night only. I have a rule.'

'Of course you do. Every girl's dream.'

Ben gave her a wry smile. 'You'd be surprised.' There
were always enough women looking for exactly that.

'So, what are you suggesting?' Luce asked.

The hint of desperation in her voice, the pleading in her
eyes, told him she was really hoping he had an answer.
She was in so deep she didn't even know how to get out.

'Stay here tonight with me, like we planned. And tomorrow, first thing, head back to Cardiff. Screw your colleague and his lecture. Forget about your family for a couple of days. You're supposed to be in Chester until Thursday, right? So no one will know you're home. You can knuckle down, sort out your book, and then spend Christmas relaxing instead of stressing out about all the work you should be doing.'

Luce's gaze darted away. 'I'm not sure I even remember how to relax.'

Ben smiled. 'Spend the night with me and I'll remind you.'

Oh, it was so, so tempting. Not just the sex—although that was bad enough. But the thought of three whole days with nothing to do except work on her book. No one asking her for anything.

Luce bit her lip. 'What about the lecture? Or my conference report? Or the Christmas Eve dinner?'

'Screw them,' Ben said, raising his glass to her. 'Decide, right here and now, that *you* are more important than what other people want from you. Decide that your book is what matters most to you at this moment in time and focus on that for the week. Make your family help you for a change. Get some priorities for once.'

He was right. The world might stop turning on its axis because of it, but he, Ben Hampton, was actually right. Maybe he'd been wrong every time he'd called her boring or obsessed at university—or maybe he hadn't been. But now he was right. She needed priorities. And maybe, if nothing else, three days alone would help her figure out what they were.

'Maybe I can get my ticket refunded. Or changed to tomorrow,' she mused. The conference organisers had bought the original ticket, but after the fiasco with her hotel room she didn't feel inclined to trust them to re-arrange her travel home. She'd head down to the station in the morning—see what they could do.

'I'll buy you a ticket,' Ben said carelessly. 'First-class. You can work on the train.'

Luce raised her eyebrows at him. 'What? As payment for services rendered? I'm not sleeping with you, remember?'

'As an apology.' Sitting up straighter, Ben fixed his gaze onto her own, and she found it impossible to look away. 'From Hampton & Sons. For losing your booking. I don't pay for sex.'

He looked more than insulted. He looked hurt. Luce's gaze darted away. 'Sorry. I didn't mean...'

'Yes, you did.' Ben sighed. 'Look. You're pretty much out of options here, Luce. I'm leaving tomorrow, and I have no doubt that this suite will be booked up for the rest of the week. You can try and find somewhere else in the city with a cancellation, or you can go home. And once you're there it's your choice whether you let anyone else know you're back.'

'Why are you doing this?' Luce asked. 'Trying to help me, I mean?' Could he possibly be so determined to get her to sleep with him that he'd try to fix her whole life to achieve it? Surely even Ben Hampton couldn't be that single-minded.

More to the point, how the hell was she meant to keep on resisting him if he was?

But Ben just shrugged. 'Because I can. Because fixing things is what I do for a living. Because it's so blatantly obvious what you need.' His words were casual, thrown away without thinking. But there was a tightness around his eyes that suggested something more.

Did he remember that night in the library? Was that what he was trying to make up for by helping her?

And, really, did it really matter? It was eight years ago. But she might never see the man again after tomorrow, and she knew the curiosity alone would drive her insane. 'Do you remember the night of your twenty-first birthday?'

Ben didn't even blink at the change of subject. 'Barely. Mostly I remember the hangover the next day. That kind of misery stays with you.'

He didn't remember. And if he didn't remember, it was as if it had never happened. She could forget it, too. Let the past go.

'I do know that I got dumped because of my actions that night.' Ben raised an eyebrow at her. 'Care to fill in the missing memories?'

Luce smiled. 'Maybe one day.' Except there wouldn't be another day, would there? Tomorrow she'd take the train home and forget all about Ben Hampton.

She tried to remind herself that this was a good thing.

Ben drained the last of his brandy and got to his feet. 'Well, I guess I'd better let you sleep on your decision. Un-less…' He gave her a hopeful look.

'I am not sleeping with you.' Whatever her rebellious body was hoping. She could feel a tightness growing in her belly just thinking about it.

He laughed, far more cheerful than she'd expected him to be about being turned down. 'In that case, if you'll ex-cuse me, I have a long drive ahead of me tomorrow.'

Bending down, he brushed a kiss against her cheek. His lips were softer than she'd imagined. Not that she'd been thinking of them.

'Goodnight, Luce.'

She watched him place his glass on the counter and

saunter into the bedroom, closing the door firmly behind him. And yet she was still staring at the door.

Her fingers brushed her cheek, as if she could trace the kiss his lips had left.

Damn him. Somehow she knew that all she'd dream about that night was what might have happened if she'd said yes.

Ben was not naturally an early riser, but his father had been, and Seb had inherited the trait, so he'd had to learn to function well before seven-thirty. And, given the motivation of breakfast with Luce before he packed her off to her new and improved existence in Cardiff, he was awake, showered and dressed before the sun was fully up the next morning. Which wasn't as impressive in December as it would have been in July, but Ben still felt a little pleased with himself as he knocked on Luce's door.

At least he was until she answered it moments later, already dressed in some sort of knitted jumper dress and those incredibly enticing boots.

He'd spent a lot of the previous evening thinking about those boots. And what Luce might be wearing under that dress. It hadn't been his most restful night's sleep ever, but his mind had at least been happily occupied.

'You're up at last, then,' Luce said, eyebrows raised.

'Were you always so smug in the mornings?' he asked as Luce wheeled her already packed suitcase into the living area. He had Seb for smugness. He really didn't need any more *smug* in his life. At least not unless he was getting to feel it for once.

'Probably.' Luce flashed him a superior smile. 'But you were mostly sleeping in while I was up working. You might not have noticed.'

Taking her suitcase and resting it against the wall by

the door, Ben decided it was time to change the subject. 'So, have you decided what you're doing today?'

Luce bit her lip. 'Heading back to Cardiff, if that offer of a train ticket still stands?'

Ben nodded. 'Of course. And when you get there?'

'I finish my book. In secret.'

A sense of relief washed over him. 'Good.' He'd done it. He might not have been able to bring his mother back from the brink before she jumped ship, but he'd fixed this. He'd fixed that little bit of Luce's life that he could influence and now he could move on, forget all about her.

That, right there, was one good day's work.

'I've ordered us breakfast,' he said, just as a knock on the door indicated its arrival.

'If nothing else, the Hampton & Sons hotel chain has certainly fed me well during my stay,' Luce said, taking a seat at the table in the dining area. 'I should write to the management.'

'I'll pass on a message.' Ben let in the room service staff member and took his own seat as platters of food were laid on the table. Eggs, bacon, toast, pastries—and plenty of hot coffee. Should keep him going on his drive through Wales, and it would make sure Luce had one more good meal before she lost herself in research and writing for the rest of the week.

'Shall I open the curtains, sir?' the room service guy asked, and Ben nodded.

Helping himself to eggs as Luce poured the coffee, Ben couldn't help but think how domestic this was. Far more couply than he'd ever managed, even with women he'd actually slept with. It was a good job she was leaving today, or she'd be straightening his tie and calling him 'honey' in no time. She was that sort.

'I'll call the station when we've eaten,' he said as light

flooded into the room from the opened curtains. 'See what times your trains are.'

But Luce wasn't listening to him. Instead she stared out of the window, coffee cup halfway to her mouth. Ben followed her gaze.

Outside, rooftops and roads were coated in a thick layer of snow, gleaming white and icy. Heavy flakes fell lazily from the sky, adding to the perfect Christmas scene.

'Huh!' Ben said, watching it fall. 'When did *that* happen?'

'I should never have gone out for dinner,' Luce muttered to herself as she waited on hold for the station. If she hadn't gone out for dinner with Ben Hampton she'd have had to try to find somewhere else to stay. When that had inevitably failed she'd have had no option but to get a train home. She'd be warm and cosy in Cardiff, watching the snow fall as she worked on her book.

Except, if she was honest with herself, she knew she wouldn't be. She'd have called her mother as soon as she got back to sort out the Christmas Eve dinner, and then she'd have been caught up in the responsibility net again. She'd be at her family's beck and call, sorting out their problems and organising their Christmas season. The book wouldn't have got a look-in.

Of course she would still have had a roof over her head, which was more than she'd have right now if the trains weren't running.

The hotel room door slammed open and shut and Ben walked back in, his hair damp with snowflakes. 'It's really not stopping out there,' he said, shrugging out of his coat. 'I spoke to Reception—apparently all trains are subject to significant delays, and a lot simply aren't running.'

Luce pressed the 'end call' button and dropped her

phone onto the sofa before perching on the arm herself.
'Fantastic.'

'You're thinking this is all my fault somehow, aren't
you?'

'Yes.' What the hell did she do now?

Ben pulled up a chair and sat opposite her. 'Okay, well,
let's see what we can do to fix this.'

Luce rolled her eyes. 'I know you pride yourself on
being able to solve problems in hotels, but I think the
British railway network might be beyond even your ca-
pabilities.'

Ben ignored her. 'Daisy on Reception says this room's
booked out for tonight, and the guest has just called to
confirm they'll still be coming, despite the snow. So that's
out. We might possibly be able to find you another room if
we get some cancellations, but there's no guarantee. Or...'

'Or?' Luce sat up a little straighter. Another option was
exactly what she needed right now. Unless, of course, this
was another Ben Hampton plan to seduce her.

'I'm driving south today anyway. Headed to my cottage down in the Brecons. Apparently it's not so bad further south just yet, and I'm confident my four-by-four can
handle it.' He shrugged. 'Wouldn't be too far out of my
way to take you on down to Cardiff. I can always stop for
the night in one of our hotels there if the snow worsens.'

Blinking at him, Luce considered. It would mean hours
in a car with Ben, on bad roads, but somehow she felt he
was a surer bet than the trains. And not even he would try
to seduce her in a snowdrift, right? 'You'd do that?'

'I still owe you for the room mix-up, remember? And
this is cheaper than a first-class train ticket, anyway.'

He made it sound like nothing, but Luce knew better.
He was fixing her life again. But if it got her home and

her book finished maybe she should just let him. Accept help for once.

Grandad hadn't had a saying to cover that one, but Luce thought there might be potential in it all the same.

'Okay, then,' she said, grabbing her phone and standing up. 'Let's go.'

# CHAPTER SIX

SOMEWHERE AROUND WELSHPOOL Ben finally admitted to himself that this might not have been the best idea he'd ever had.

The integral sat nav in the car had wanted him to cross over the border and drive south through England, before nipping back into Wales just before Cardiff. But Ben had done the drive south through Wales to the Brecons and the cottage enough times to feel confident in his route, and he didn't need advice for the uninitiated. Besides, the travel news had reported a pile-up on the A49 that would make things incredibly tedious, so really a drive through the hills had been the only option.

Right now, though, he'd take a three-hour traffic jam over these roads.

Daisy on the front desk had assured him that the snow was worst in the north. What she hadn't mentioned was that it was heading south. Every mile of their journey had been undertaken with snow clouds hovering above, keeping pace, and dumping more of the white stuff in their path as they drove.

Ben's arms ached from gripping the steering wheel tightly enough to yank the car back under control as the road twisted and slipped under them. His eyes felt gritty from staring into the falling snow, trying to see the path ahead. And Luce was not helping at all.

To start with she'd just looked tense. Then her hands had balled up against her thighs. Then she'd grabbed onto the seat, knuckles white. Ben had stopped looking over at her as the road grew more treacherous, but he'd bet money that she had a look of terror on her face now.

'Are you sure this is the best way to go?' Luce asked, her voice a little faint.

'Yes.' At least at this point it was pretty much the only option.

'Do you think…? Is the snow getting heavier?'

'No.' Except it was. Any idiot could see that. But the last thing Ben needed was Luce freaking out on him in the middle of a snowstorm.

'Are you just saying that to make me feel better?'

That sounded more like the Luce he'd had dinner with last night. Sharp and insightful.

'Yes.'

'Thought so.' She took a breath and released her death grip on the seat. 'Okay. What do you need me to do?'

'Keep quiet and don't freak out.' Ben ground the words out. Distraction was dangerous.

'Okay. I can do that.'

He wasn't sure if she was reassuring herself or him, but she did seem to relax a little. At least until they hit the Brecon Beacons National Park.

As the car climbed the hills the skies darkened even further, looking more like night than afternoon. The falling flakes doubled in size, until his windscreen wipers couldn't keep up, and the slow progress he'd been making dropped to a crawl. The road ahead had disappeared into a mist of white and the hills were blending into the sky.

They were never going to make it to Cardiff tonight.

'Okay. New plan.' Running through the road systems in his head, Ben prodded a couple of buttons on the sat nav and decided that maybe, just this once, he'd take its advice. Anything that got him off these roads, out of this car and somewhere warm. Preferably with a large drink.

'What? Where are we going?' Luce peered at the sat nav, which was insistently telling him to turn right. 'We need to get to Cardiff!'

'We're never going to make Cardiff in this.' Ben swung the car slowly to the right and hoped he'd hit an actual road. 'We need to get somewhere safe until this passes.'

'Like where?' Luce asked, her tone rising in incredulity.

'My cottage,' Ben reminded her. 'It's a damn sight closer than Cardiff, and a lot safer than these roads.'

There was silence from the passenger seat. When Ben finally risked a glance over, Luce was staring at him. 'What?'

'You planned this,' she said, her words firm and full of conviction. 'This was the plan all along.'

'Getting stuck in a snowstorm? I know I'm a powerful man, Luce, but the weather's up there with the rail network on the list of things I can't control.'

'That's why we came this way. You *knew* the snow would be bad, so you planned to kidnap me and take me to your cottage. You're still mad I wouldn't sleep with you last night.'

Was the woman actually insane?

'Trust me—sleeping with you is the last thing on my mind right now. I'm more concerned with us—oh, I don't know—not dying.'

'I should have taken the train.' The words were muffled as Luce buried her mouth into the long fluffy scarf wrapped around her neck.

'Next time I'll let you,' Ben promised, relief seeping

through him as he made out enough letters on the next road sign to reassure him they were nearly at the village nearest his cottage. Two more turns and they'd be there. Once they got onto the last rocky upward track. 'Hold on,' he warned her. Then he took a breath and turned the wheel.

Luce had never liked rollercoasters. Or fairground rides. Or ferries, actually. And the journey through the hills with Ben had felt far too much like all three for her liking. Rising and falling, rocking, swaying in the wind... She could feel breakfast threatening to rise up in her throat as they bumped over the rocky track Ben had just violently swerved up.

All she wanted was to be at home. Warm, safe and merrily lost in the Middle Ages. Was that so much to ask?

But instead she was...*where*, exactly? Somewhere in the Brecon Beacons, she supposed. Risking her life on an unsafe track to get to Ben's love-nest in the hills. Somewhere to wait out the storm and focus very hard on reasons not to indulge in a one-night stand with Ben.

Suddenly Cardiff felt a very long way away.

The car jerked to a halt and Luce rubbed at her collarbone where the seatbelt dug in.

'We're here.' Ben threw open the door and jumped out into the snow, as if any amount of cold were better than being stuck in the car with her.

He was still mad about her suspicions, then. And, yes, okay—rationally she knew he probably hadn't intended this to happen and couldn't actually control the snow.

But it was still all a little too convenient and willpower-testing for her liking.

Unfastening her seatbelt, Luce followed, stepping gingerly into the soft piles of snow and wishing she'd packed more practical boots. Peering through the snow, she followed Ben's tracks up what she presumed must be a path under all the white and saw, at last, Ben's cottage.

Luce wasn't sure what she'd expected, exactly. Maybe a collection of holiday chalets attached to a hotel. Or an os-tentatious, look-how-rich-I-am manor house sort of thing that could only be called a cottage ironically. Whatever it was, it wasn't this. An actual, honest-to-God stone cot-tage in the hills.

It was perfect.

'Come on,' Ben said, and she realised the front door was open. 'If you freeze to death you'll never forgive me.'

'True,' Luce said, and hurried in after him.

With the door closed fast behind them, the wild winds and swirling snow seemed suddenly miles away. It wasn't hot in the cottage, by any means, but it was warm at least. Ben turned his attention immediately to the stone fireplace that dominated the lounge, stacking sticks and paper with practised ease.

Luce stared around her, taking in the unexpected sur-roundings. It certainly wasn't the sort of space she'd imag-ined Ben feeling comfortable in. Yes, it had a modern open-plan layout, but there were none of the bright white surfaces and stainless-steel accessories she'd expected, even after seeing the rustic outlook of the place. Instead the large main room was decorated in earthy colours—warming, welcoming reds and browns and greens. The battered leather sofas had tawny throw blankets and cush-ions on them—perfect for curling up in front of the fire. And the sheepskin rug before the fireplace made even the grey stone floor more warming.

Not Ben. Not at all.

'When did you buy this place?' she asked, stripping off her coat and scarf and hanging them over the back of a kitchen chair before removing her boots.

'A couple of years ago. I wanted somewhere separate. Somewhere that was mine.'

Luce thought she could understand that. Of course she encouraged her family to treat her house as theirs, but technically it belonged to her. That mattered.

'Did you get someone in to decorate?' Because this was the perfect rustic-cottage look. The sort of thing that either happened naturally or cost thousands via an interior designer. She didn't see Ben as the naturally rustic type.

'I did it,' Ben said, without looking up from the tiny flame he was coaxing.

Luce tried to hide her surprise. 'Well, it's gorgeous,' she said after a moment. Because it was—even more so, somehow, now she knew it was his own work. It wasn't beautiful, or tasteful, or on trend. It was warm and cosy and she loved it.

As the fire caught Ben flashed her a smile—the first she'd seen since they left Chester.

'So glad you approve.'

In that moment the cottage itself ceased to be the most attractive thing in the vicinity. Luce swallowed, looked away and said, 'Um…so, how long do you think we'll be stuck here?'

Standing up, Ben straightened, brushing his hands off on his jeans. 'Until the snow stops, at least. Don't think we'll be going anywhere until tomorrow.'

Tomorrow. Which meant spending another night in close proximity to Ben Hampton. Another night of not throwing caution to the wind and saying, *Seduce me.* Just to find out, after eight years of wondering, what it would be like.

The look he gave her suggested that he'd read her mind—but imperfectly. 'Don't fret. There's a spare room. It even has a key to lock it from the inside, if you're still worried that this is some great master plan to get into your knickers.'

Heat flushed in Luce's cheeks. She should probably apologise for that at some point. But since he was the one who'd point-blank propositioned her the night before maybe sorry could wait. Besides, just as the night before, she was more concerned that she'd need the lock to keep herself in, rather than him out.

*Not thinking about it.*

'What do we do until then?' she asked.

Ben shrugged. 'Up to you. Work, if you like. Personally, I'm going to make myself an Irish coffee and warm up by the fire. Then, once this snow slows down, I'm going to walk down into the village and see if the Eight Bells is serving dinner. I'd invite you to join me, but I'd hate for you to get the wrong idea about my intentions.'

'I do still need to eat,' Luce pointed out. 'And besides, Hampton & Sons have once again failed to make good on their promise—I was supposed to be in Cardiff by now. The way I figure it, you owe me another dinner.'

Ben raised an eyebrow. 'Really? Seems to me that you relying on me for a bed for the night—without, I might add, any of the activities that usually make such a thing worthwhile—is becoming a bit of a habit. So, is that dinner *instead* of a night's free accommodation in a charmingly rustic cottage?'

Luce considered. 'Maybe we could go halves on dinner?'

'Good plan.' Ben moved into the kitchen area and pulled a bag of coffee from the cupboard. 'So, do you want the grand tour?'

Luce spun round to smile at him and nodded. 'Yes, please.'

'Right, then.' Waving an arm expansively around the

living, dining and kitchen space, he said, 'This is the main room. Bathroom's over there. That's my room. That's yours.' He pointed at the relevant doors in turn. 'Back door leads out to the mountain. Front door leads to the car and a lot of snow. That's about it. Now, how Irish do you want your coffee?'

She should take advantage of the afternoon to work, really. But her laptop was still in the car, and she was cold and tired and stuck with Ben Hampton for another night. She deserved a warming drink and a sit by the fire, didn't she?

Luce perched on a kitchen stool and watched him fill the coffee maker. 'Make sure it's at least got a decent accent.'

Ben grinned at her. 'Will do.'

Ben had been more concerned with getting in and getting warm than studying Luce's expression when they arrived at the cottage. But now, watching her sink into the sofa, coffee in hand and feet stretched out towards the fire, he smiled to see her looking so at home there.

It wasn't an impressive cottage. He knew that. None of the homes in a ten-mile radius had more than three bedrooms; anything bigger would have been ostentatious. Ben wanted to fit in here. So when he'd bought the tumble-down stone building he hadn't extended it, just rebuilt it as it would have been. And it wasn't the most expensive of his properties—not by a long stretch. But it was his favourite. Not least because it was the only one that was really *his*. Bought with his own money, chosen by himself, decorated by himself. The penthouse in London, impressive as it was, belonged to the company and had been decorated by their interior designer. And the château... That still had his grandmother's favourite rose print wallpaper all over it. He really needed to get out there and start sorting that place out.

But not now. This was his week off. His week of relaxation in his favourite place. Albeit with an unexpected, suspicious and snappish guest, and the prospect of a round trip to Cardiff in the snow tomorrow.

Sipping his own coffee, Ben let the warmth of the cottage flood his bones, relax his muscles, the way it always did when he came home.

*Home.* Luce had asked him where it was and he'd said he didn't have one. He hadn't explained that he didn't want one. He'd had a home once, only to lose it when his father's obsession with work drove his mother away.

He didn't need a home that could be taken from him. He just needed a bolthole to hide out and recharge. Could be anywhere. Right now it just happened to be here, that was all.

*I need to spend more time here.*

Once he'd deposited Luce home he'd come back and look at his work schedule for the next twelve months. Figure out where there might be a break long enough to get back to Wales again. Maybe even over to France.

Luce drained her coffee and said, 'So, this pub you mentioned?'

'The Eight Bells. Best pint and best pies this side of the border.' They'd missed lunch in the snow. She was probably as starving as he was.

'Sounds promising,' Luce said, but she didn't sound convinced.

Ben decided to put her out of her misery. 'And, for you townies, there's a pretty decent wine list, too.'

'Oh, thank God.' Her face brightened.

Ben chuckled. 'Less than a day with me and you're already desperate for a drink? What? The coffee not Irish enough for you?'

'It's lovely,' Luce said. 'But after this day I'm ready for a hearty meal and a large glass of wine.'

Ben enjoyed one more moment of warmth by the fire, then got to his feet. 'In that case, I guess we'd better prepare to face the elements again. You ready?'

Luce grinned and took his hand to let him pull her up. 'As I'll ever be.'

# CHAPTER SEVEN

AFTER A SNOWY, freezing and downright treacherous walk into the village, Luce stamped the snow off her boots, unwound her scarf and let Ben go and find menus and drinks while she settled into a chair at the rustic wood table by an inglenook fireplace. The Eight Bells was certainly a lot nicer than she'd expected in a local village pub, but then, she supposed they were in the heart of tourist Wales around here. Made sense to cater to the townies.

Not that there were many of them around tonight. Only a handful of tables were occupied, and those were by locals discussing the weather and when the roads would be cleared.

She shouldn't have been surprised that Ben would find a cottage near fine dining and local shops that delivered organic produce, she supposed. That was just who he was. How had she forgotten that?

It was the cottage, she decided. It was so homely. Somewhere she could imagine actually living herself. Nothing like the fancy hotel he'd been living in when she and Mandy had visited from university. Not even anything like the suite at the Royal Court in Chester. And yet it was his. Maybe there were nuances to Ben Hampton she was missing after all.

'Check out the pie list.' Ben dropped a couple of menus

on the table, then placed a glass of white wine in front of her. Wrapping her fingers round the stem, she took a long sip. Ben was right; this place had really good wine.

'You recommend the pies, then?' she asked, scanning the menu.

'I recommend everything on the menu.' He wasn't even looking at it, she realised.

'You come here often?'

'As often as I can.' He sipped his pint. 'The owner's an old friend of mine.'

That was one constant. Ben had always had a lot of friends around. When Mandy had started dating him Luce had assumed that his hangers-on were after his money, or the parties he could get them into. But over time it had become clear that they genuinely enjoyed his company. Ben was one of those people with a talent for making people like him.

Not a talent Luce had ever claimed to possess.

'I'll try the chicken pie, then,' she said, closing the menu. Ben nodded, and went to place their order. Watching him go, Luce studied the width of his shoulders, the confidence of his stride. Apart from a little extra muscle and size, how much had he really changed in the last eight years? Was he still the same boy who had kissed her in the hotel library?

Would he try again?

He was back before she had anything approaching an answer to that question.

'So,' he said, settling himself into his chair with practised ease, 'Old Joe over there tells me the snow should be over for now, but we might get another load tomorrow night. Hopefully the roads will be clear enough tomorrow to make a break for Cardiff before it hits. A few of the locals plan to take the tractors out in the morning and clear them.'

'That's good.' Getting home tomorrow would still give her a day and a half to work, at the least.

'Until then I'm afraid you're stuck with me. So, in the meantime, I believe this is the part where we make small talk. What topic do you want? Politics? Religion?'

'Tell me what you've been doing since university.' He looked surprised, so she added, 'I bored you about Nest last night. Now it's your turn.'

She needed to know where he'd been, what he'd done, so she could understand who he was now. For some reason it seemed vitally important that she make sense of him before they headed back to the cottage and their separate beds. Luce very carefully ignored the small part of her brain that murmured, *And if I understand him, if I know him, I'll know if it's safe to ask him to kiss me tonight.*

But Ben just shrugged and said, 'Pretty much as expected. Graduated and went to work for the family business...'

'It seems to be doing well enough.'

His smile was a trifle smug. 'Doubled the profits in my first five years. On track to triple them in the next two.'

*That* Ben was familiar. The one who thought money was the most important thing in the world. 'Your father must be very proud,' she said, thinking of the stern grey-haired man she'd met that one fateful day she'd spent in Ben's world. She didn't mean it to sound so dry, so sarcastic, but it came out that way regardless.

'He died about a year ago.' Ben's eyes were on his glass rather than her as he spoke, and a sharp spike of sympathy pierced Luce's chest.

'I'm so sorry.' She knew how that felt. That hole—the

space where a person should be. Trying to find a way to live without someone who'd defined you all your life.

But Ben rolled his shoulders back and gave her a strange half-smile. 'I wouldn't be. To be honest, I've barely noticed the difference. Just means that now it's my brother Seb checking up on my methods instead.'

There he was. The boy who'd had so little regard for the things that mattered—family, friends, responsibility, doing the right thing—had grown up exactly as she'd expected. Into a man who still had no respect for the things that mattered to her. A man she couldn't consider sleeping with even if she was sure it would be magnificent. *And* a sure way to find that relaxation he promised.

Except there was something in his eyes. Something else. 'You must miss him, though?'

'He wasn't really the sort of father you missed.'

She wanted to ask more, to try to understand how his father's death could have had so little impact on him. But before she could find the right question the waitress brought their food and Ben had switched the conversation to pies and homemade chips.

In fact, Luce realised as she tucked into her truly delicious meal, he seemed almost too keen to keep the conversation light and inconsequential. As he started another story about a hotel somewhere in Scotland that had served compulsory haggis to its guests for breakfast every Sunday Luce smiled politely, nodded in the right places and tried to think of a way to get him to open up. He was hiding something, she was sure, and her incurable curiosity was determined to find out what it was before she had to return to Cardiff.

'Let's have another drink before we head home,' she suggested, when he paused in regaling her with his tales.

*Home.* Oh, God, she'd just called the cottage 'home'. If

ever anything was guaranteed to send a man running in the opposite direction, laying claim to his house as your own before you'd even really been on a proper date was probably it. But Ben hadn't flinched or reacted. Maybe he hadn't noticed. Maybe Luce really could be that lucky.

'Sure. But I warn you now: I'm not carrying you back in that snow.'

'I think I can manage.'

Ben studied her carefully, as if he suspected an ulterior motive, but at least he didn't seem terrified at her presumption. Luce tried not to shift under his gaze and pretended very hard that she'd said nothing of consequence at all.

'Okay, then.' Ben got to his feet. 'You have a look at the pudding menu while I get the drinks.'

Now, *that* was a mission Luce could get stuck into. Then all she had to do was figure out a way to get Ben to open up to her.

Ben rested his weight against the bar, waiting for their drinks, and watched Luce from the corner of his eye. Not that she'd notice. She seemed completely absorbed by the dessert menu, and he wondered if she'd go for the chocolate mousse or the sticky toffee pudding. She didn't seem like a fruit salad girl. It was one of the things he liked about her.

That was a surprise in itself. The Lucinda he'd known so many years ago hadn't been someone you liked. She hadn't let anyone close enough to find out any of her likable qualities. Locked up in her room studying, running off to the library or covering the tiny kitchen table in the flat with papers and textbooks. That was how he remembered her. The way she'd always run off to her room when he and Mandy had arrived home. Apart from a few hastily eaten dinners together, when Mandy insisted on them 'getting to know each other', that was all he'd known of her. He'd never been able to understand how someone as outgoing and fun-loving as Mandy could even be friends with her. Hadn't believed her when she'd said that Luce could be fun sometimes.

He could see it now, though. She was the sort of woman who grew into herself. Her confidence and self-possession had let her beauty, humour and personality shine out at last. And she'd grown into her body, too. Had she grown into her sexuality in the same way?

It bothered him how much he wanted to find out.

And now the weather had given him the perfect chance to do just that. It might not have been a plan in the way Luce had accused him, but it certainly was an opportunity to take advantage of.

One night in a secluded cottage was even more perfect than one night in a luxury hotel. As long as it was just one night and the snow didn't strand them there any longer. Two nights in a row and women started to get ideas, Ben had found. Which was why he'd committed to his one-night rule.

And Luce was up to something; that much was clear. Given another glass of wine, he was pretty sure he could figure out what, and how it might affect his seduction plans.

The barmaid handed over their drinks and Ben took them with a wide, friendly smile before heading back to Luce. He had hopes for what was going on here, and if he was right the evening could be set for a much better ending than he'd dared to assume the night before.

'So, what are you fancying?' Ben put the drinks down on the table and tried not to smirk when Luce looked up, eyes wide and face flustered.

'Um…' Her gaze flicked back down to the menu. 'The sticky toffee pudding?'

'Good choice.' Dropping into his chair, Ben reached his arms out across the back and felt his muscles stretch. 'Tracy says she'll be over to take our order in a moment.'

'Great.' Placing the menu back on the table, Luce folded her hands over it.

Ben braced himself for whatever line of questioning was coming next.

'So, what do you do when you're not working?'

To his horror, Ben actually had to think about an answer. When had he become so obsessed with work? That was Seb and Dad. Not him.

'Oh, you know. The usual. Fine dining. Trips abroad.' That sounded obnoxious. She already thought he was obnoxious. He really shouldn't make it any worse. 'I have a château in France—well, my grandmother did. She left it to me. I'm renovating it.' Or he should be. He *would* be. As soon as he found the time.

Luce raised her eyebrows and Ben cast his gaze over to the bar to see where the hell Tracy the barmaid had got to.

'You're interested in property development? First the cottage, now the château?'

'Yes,' Ben lied. It had nothing to do with making money. He'd done up the cottage so he had somewhere to escape to. And he wanted to do the château because…well, he couldn't just leave it there to crumble, now, could he?

'So what's next?' Luce asked, then glanced up and said, 'Oh, the sticky toffee pudding for me, please.'

It took Ben a moment to catch up, to realise that Tracy was standing patiently behind him with her notebook. 'Same for me, please.' He gave her a smile and watched her walk back to the bar. Maybe Luce would get cross enough at him paying attention to another woman that she'd stop asking questions he didn't want to answer.

No such luck.

'So?' she repeated. 'What comes after the château?'

'No idea,' Ben said with a shrug. 'You know me—I'm a take-one-day-at-a-time kind of guy.'

Except he wasn't any more. Not really. He couldn't be—not when Seb was relying on him so much these days. He knew exactly what would be next. More visits to more hotels. More reports on what was working and what wasn't. Long, long meetings with Seb and his team about where the company was going. More spot inspections on long-standing members of the Hampton & Sons chain. More firing old managers and putting in their own people. More budget meetings where the accountants told them they should get the hotels to improve drastically without giving them any money to do it.

Business was business, after all.

'Still?' Luce asked. 'I suppose I shouldn't be surprised. People don't really change at heart, do they?'

Ben looked at her, sipping her wine across the table, her gaze too knowing, and for once he wanted to tell someone the truth. That sometimes he was sick of all the rules he'd set for himself. That sometimes he did want to stop. To stay in one place for a while.

Downing the rest of his pint, he said, 'I need another drink,' and headed to the bar before the urge became too strong.

# CHAPTER EIGHT

BEN RETURNED WITH another pint for himself and another glass of wine for Luce. She hadn't drunk more than half of the glass she already had, but she accepted it gracefully anyway. She had a feeling that he wasn't so much trying to get her drunk to take advantage of her, more to distract her.

Clearly he'd never experienced the Myles curiosity in full flow before.

'So, you left university, joined the family business, and you're still there?' She tipped her head sideways to look at him. 'So either you really have changed a little bit, or there's something about your job you truly love. Because the Ben Hampton I knew couldn't stick at anything for more than six months.' Which had, incidentally, been the exact length of his relationship with Mandy before the kiss in the library. Not that she'd counted.

Ben's hand was already on his pint. 'It's a job. It pays me very, very well and I don't have to sit in an office all day.'

Now, *that* sounded like the Ben she'd known. But it still felt wrong, somehow. And Luce had drunk enough wine to tell him so. 'That doesn't sound like it makes you happy.'

'Are jobs supposed to make you happy?' Ben asked, eyebrow raised.

'Mine does,' Luce said, in an immediate unconsidered response.

'Really?'

'Of course.' At least as long as she didn't think too much about the particulars. A lecturing position at the university and the opportunity to do her own research into areas of history that fascinated her. That was all she'd ever wanted.

It was just that day-to-day, dealing with the academic system, the obscure rules and regulations of academia, funding, and other colleagues...well, it could be a little... frustrating.

'So, which part do you love the most?' Ben asked. 'Attending dull lectures your colleagues can't be bothered to go to? Grading unoriginal essays? Applying for funding all the time just to actually do your job?'

Which was just a bit too close to her own thoughts for Luce's comfort. 'I'm not saying there aren't downsides, or days that aren't particularly joyous. But at the heart of it I love discovering the past. I love finding out about the lives of women long dead and how they influenced the world around them. That's what matters to me.'

Ben's gaze was curious now. How had this got turned around? Wasn't *she* supposed to be questioning *him*?

'In that case,' he asked, 'why aren't you spending all your time on your book? Looking at a linked lecture tour or even a TV programme? Why are you wasting time writing reports for your lazy colleague?'

'This is just how it works,' Luce said, reaching for her glass as an excuse not to look at him. 'It can't be all fun, all the time. There has to be responsibility, too.'

'And that's why I'm still working for the family business,' Ben said. 'Told you I could be responsible sometimes. Ah, look—pudding.'

Tracy put their bowls on the table with a curious glance between them. How many women had he brought here? Luce wondered. Was she the latest in a long line? Did she not fit the usual stereotype? Was that why everyone kept looking at her tonight?

She couldn't think about that now. What did it matter, anyway? Tomorrow she'd be back in Cardiff. She'd probably never think of Ben Hampton again.

*Liar.*

'Okay, then,' she said, reaching for her spoon. 'What would you be doing if you weren't working for the illustrious Hampton & Sons?'

Ben's spoon paused halfway to his mouth. 'Honestly? I have no idea.' He looked as if the concept had never even occurred to him. As if he'd never thought about what he'd actually *like* to do. He'd just fallen into his job and kept going.

Which was so entirely out of keeping with what Luce had thought she knew about his character that she forgot about pudding entirely.

'Well, what do you love doing?' she asked. 'Renovating properties?'

'I suppose.' He put his spoon back in his bowl and looked at her. 'Look, you seem to have the wrong impression here. I am very good at my job, and it serves the purpose I want it to serve—namely paying me more than enough to enjoy my life. Doing my job well keeps my brother and the investors happy. And I get to live my life my way. I never wanted my job to be my life, so this arrangement suits me pretty much perfectly.'

Explanation over, he dug back into his sticky toffee pudding and ignored Luce completely.

Which was fine by her. No need for him to see the utter confusion she was sure was painted across her face.

She just couldn't get a handle on this man. Every time she thought she understood something—that he'd changed, that he hadn't—he pulled the rug out again. Just when she was sure that he was a man stuck in a job he hated, search-ing for something to fulfil him, he turned round and told her that was the last thing he wanted.

She just didn't understand.

'You're looking baffled,' Ben said.

Luce glanced up to see him smiling in amusement. 'Just...trying to understand.'

His mouth took a sympathetic downturn, but his eyes were still laughing. 'I know. It's always hard for over-achievers to understand that work isn't everything.'

'That's not... There are plenty of things in my life be-sides work.'

'Oh, of course. Like running around after your family and friends, making their lives run smoothly.'

'Aren't you doing the same for your brother?'

Ben shook his head. 'Not at all. My job is my job, and I am compensated very handsomely for it, thank you.'

'There isn't a price you can put on love.'

'No,' Ben said, his voice suddenly, shockingly hard. 'There isn't. But what you do for them? That isn't love. That's pandering.'

Luce's emotions swung back again. No, he hadn't changed. Not at all. He still thought that he and his thoughts, his wants, his opinions, were the only things in the world that mattered. Couldn't begin to imagine that he might be wrong. That it might be different for other people.

'No—listen to me.'

Ben reached out and grabbed her hand with his own as he spoke, and Luce looked up into unexpectedly seri-ous eyes.

'What do you want more than anything in the world?'

His skin against hers. His attention firmly placed on her. Those were the only reasons she felt a jolt of lust through her body at his question. The only reason her mind answered, *You.*

Luce pulled her hand away. *Note to self: I do not want to sleep with this man. It would be disastrous.*

'I want my family to be happy. Settled.' Because, she admitted, to herself if not out loud, if they were—if they didn't need her so damn much—maybe she could go out and find what made *her* happy.

'Because that would set you free?' Ben said.

Luce's gaze shot to his in surprise.

'Because if they were happy you wouldn't have to worry about them. But, Luce, they're never going to be happy and settled without you as long as you're still there bailing them out at every turn. You'll give and give until there's nothing of you left. And then you'll crack. My mother—' He stopped, looked away. 'I've seen it before. You can't give up your own life for your family.'

Luce swallowed. 'You have no idea what you're talking about.'

'I think I do.' The words were bitter.

But he didn't. And Luce couldn't tell him. How could she explain a grandfather who'd worked hard all his life for the little he had to a man who'd been born with everything? How could she explain the importance of doing the best job she could, giving it everything she had so she could be proud of herself at the end of the day? His job meant nothing to Ben, was just a means to an end. It was all about the money. So how could she explain the passion she felt when she uncovered a hidden bit of women's history? When she brought untold stories to light?

'You don't. My grandfather's last words to me... He made me promise to take care of my family. I'm the only one, you see. My mother's a wonderful woman, but she's lost in her own world most of the time. And my brother and sister inherited that. They don't see the real world. None of them do. That's why they need me.'

'They're not your responsibility.'

Ben's voice was gentle, but the words still stung.

'And maybe it's time for a change. For them to learn to look after themselves.'

Luce shook her head. 'I told you. They are what they are. They're not going to change now.'

'Not if you don't give them the chance.'

That wasn't fair. 'People don't change. Not really.'

'Not even you?' Ben asked, eyebrow raised.

Luce laughed. 'Especially not me. I'm exactly the same Lucinda Myles you remember from university, right?'

Ben's gaze trailed slowly across her face, down her body, and Luce felt her blood warm.

'Not exactly the same.'

'That's not the point. My family are my responsibility, whatever you think.' Because they were all she had, too. And wasn't that a sad thing, at twenty-eight, to have nothing else but a family that needed you? Luce drained the last of her wine. 'I think it's time to go home,' she said, and Ben nodded.

They were halfway to the cottage before she realised she'd called it 'home' again.

They walked back to the cottage in silence. The snow had stopped, at last, but the paths were still slippery underfoot. The air stung Ben's lungs as they climbed the path, making it too painful to talk even if he'd had any idea of what to say.

Why was she so entrenched in solving things for her family? Because she'd promised her grandfather? That didn't seem enough. There had to be something else, but he was damned if he could figure out what. When would she learn? You couldn't fix everything for anyone. So you did what you could and you moved on. You couldn't let other people pull you down.

Had she been like this at university? He couldn't remember. She must have gone home a lot, though, since he and Mandy had often taken advantage of the flat being empty at weekends. A sliver of self-loathing jarred into him. Of course *that* was what he remembered. Why hadn't he paid more attention to Luce then?

Or perhaps the better question was, why was he paying so much attention to her now?

Finally they reached the cottage and Ben dug in his pockets for the keys. Luce waited silently at his side for the door to open. Inside, the under-floor heating was doing its job admirably, which was just as well as the fire had all but burnt out. They both stripped off their outer layers, and Ben took the coats and hung them by the back door. When he turned round Luce still stood where he'd left her, looking at him, her eyes huge and sad.

'Do you really believe that your family aren't your responsibility?'

She looked distraught at the idea that anyone could believe such a thing. *She should have spent some time with my old man.*

He wanted to say the right thing. Words that would make her smile again, as she had over dinner. But he wasn't going to lie to her.

'I think that your family need to learn to manage without you for a while. You can't mortgage your own life, your own happiness, for theirs.'

Luce just shook her head. 'We really haven't changed at all, have we?'

Despite her assertions that people didn't change, she sounded so forlorn at the idea that Ben moved closer, his body determined to comfort her even if his mind knew it was a bad idea. His hands settled at her waist as she spoke again.

'We're exactly the same people we were at university.'

'No.' Even to his own ears his voice sounded harsh. 'We're not.'

Luce looked up at him. She was so close that he could see the uncertainty in her eyes.

'Aren't we? I may not wear jeans and baggy jumpers every day, but I'd still rather be working than in the pub. Tonight notwithstanding,' she added, a small smile on her lips.

'You came to the pub, though. That's new.'

'Maybe. And what about you? Back then...'

'I spent every night in the pub and didn't care about work,' Ben finished for her. 'I promise you that tonight is not representative of my adult life.'

'Back then,' Luce repeated, 'you cared about yourself first. Your own happiness was most important, and you didn't want the responsibility of anyone else's on your shoulders.'

A memory struck him—something long forgotten and hidden. A book-lined room and a dark-haired girl in the moonlight, a plain dress draped over her body, fear and confusion in her eyes as he moved closer. Had that really been him? No wonder Mandy had ditched him. He hadn't cared about Luce's happiness then, had he? Or the respon-sibility he had to his girlfriend. *Hell.* Did Luce remem-ber? She must. That was why she'd asked. No wonder she needed to know if he'd changed.

'I care enough about you to try and help you finish your book. Reclaim your life.' He was grasping at straws, he knew. Trying to find something to show her he *had* changed.

Luce tipped her head to the side. 'Do you? Or are you just trying to get me into bed?'

'I can't do both?' Ben joked, but Luce's face was serious. He sighed. 'Trust me, I wouldn't do all of this just for sex.' He pulled away, but her hand brushed his arm, a silent request to stay close, and despite the desperate urge to leave this conversation behind and retreat to his room with a bottle of whisky, Ben found he couldn't move.

'I have to know. Do you really not remember your twenty-first? Are you sure you're not trying to make up for that night?'

Ben shook his head automatically. It hadn't even occurred to him that he should.

'Or finish what you started?'

'I didn't even remember until just now. I…I knew I hadn't been kind to you back then. Maybe that was why I took you to dinner last night. Gave you somewhere to stay. This is something entirely different.'

Her teeth sank into her lower lip as she stepped forward, closer than before, so close that he could feel her breath through the cotton of his shirt. She looked up, her eyes bright, and Ben felt his breath catch in his chest.

'Then the only thing I can think is that you wanted me here so you could hear me beg you to seduce me.'

*God, yes.* Heat flooded through his body at her words, fierce and unchecked. Her lashes fluttered shut over her eyes and Ben knew this was his chance. This was the closest she'd let herself get to asking for what she wanted. This was the moment he should sweep her up in his arms and off to bed, like Owain kidnapping Nest.

And he couldn't.

He couldn't be what she remembered—alcohol on his breath as he pushed a kiss on her, whether she wanted it or not. He was a different man now, and she needed to know that. People really did change.

Stepping back caused him physical pain. His muscles were aching to stay with her, to pull her against his chest and hold her close.

'Not like this,' he said, his voice hoarse.

And then he walked away.

# CHAPTER NINE

Luce woke up on Wednesday morning determined not to spend one more sleepless night on Ben Hampton.

She was through. From nights spent waiting for him and Mandy to kick everyone else out of the flat and go to bed at university, to the long, long night after she ran away from him in the hotel library, to that night in Chester, to last night, spent wondering and wondering. It was enough.

It didn't matter if he'd changed his mind about seducing her. In fact it was a good thing that he hadn't. Because the very last thing Luce needed at the moment was someone else needing her to take care of their lives. She had a book to write, after all, and Ben Hampton's life was a mess—even if he was too busy trying to fix hers to notice it.

Actually, she told herself, staring up at the uneven ceiling of the cottage, it was probably all for the best. She'd made a decision eight years ago not to get involved with this man. A decision she'd renewed and confirmed in Chester, and again yesterday when he brought her to the cottage. She might have nearly broken that resolution because of too much wine and conversation, or because of a brief, misguided hope that people really could change, but that wasn't enough. She should thank Ben, really, for *not* taking advantage of her vulnerable position and letting her stick to her beliefs.

Not that she was going to, of course.

Shifting under the sheet, Luce turned over with a sigh. The problem was that she wanted him. She might not be the most obviously sexual person in the world—but she was an academic, not a nun. Although they might as well be the same thing at the moment. Too much time working, researching, writing, lecturing… It didn't leave a lot of time for romance. Or even just a fun encounter with a gorgeous guy.

But Luce wasn't supposed to want that, was she? It wasn't the way she was made. Wasn't in her history. No, she was supposed to study, to learn, to improve herself. Sex didn't improve anything in her admittedly limited experience. Hell, even Nest, in her restricted, disapproving time, had managed to have more sex with considerably more guys than Luce had.

Her head flopped back against the pillow and she finally admitted the truth to herself. She'd wanted Ben Hampton last night. And, more than that, she'd wanted him to make the first move—to take her—so that she could rationalise away her desire this morning. She'd wanted to be able to say it was a weak moment, that it was the wine and the romantic snowbound cottage. She'd wanted to be able to move on and forget it without admitting that sex with him was something she really wanted.

Craved. Needed.

Well, she was just going to have to get used to going without. Because there was no way she could ask him for it now. Humiliation really wasn't her colour, and she wouldn't risk him turning her down again.

*Damn it.*

With a deep breath, Luce sat up. 'Time to move on,' she said softly.

Her room—the spare room—had a desk, a king-sized

bed and an *en suite* bathroom. If you had to be stranded in the middle of nowhere, Luce figured this was the sort of place you wanted to be stuck. It wasn't a particularly feminine room, but then, Luce wouldn't have expected it to be. Ben had decorated it, after all. The huge bed was draped in a wine-red quilt, soft and cosy, with cushions and pillows piled up at the head. Beside the bed stood a chenille-covered armchair, perfect for curling up with a book. And under the window was the desk—sturdy, probably antique, and exactly what she needed. Slipping out of bed, Luce ran a hand across its scarred wooden surface and for the first time could imagine herself finishing her book. Telling Nest's story to the world, finally, the way she wanted it to be known.

Might as well make the best of a bad situation. She was stuck there at least until Ben woke up. She'd retrieved her laptop from the car before their trip to the pub, so she could at least get some work done.

Luce listened for movement outside her door and, hearing nothing, risked slipping out long enough to make a pot of tea and some toast and sneak it back into her room. Then, wrapped up in her pyjamas, socks and an old jumper she'd found in one of the drawers, she settled down at her desk.

Ben Hampton didn't matter any more. All that did matter was telling Nest's story the right way.

There was no sign of Luce when Ben emerged from his room the next morning. Which was probably for the best. His surge of nobility, admittedly spurred on by a determination to prove that he *had* changed in the last eight years, might not have lasted in the face of Luce in pyjamas. Or a nightdress. Or maybe nothing at all...

After a night of contemplating the possibilities, and

imagining what might have happened if he'd just kissed her properly and carried her off to bed, those images were firmly burned onto his brain. God only knew what it was going to take to get them out again. And knowing she was just metres away, probably still in bed, really wasn't helping.

Ben eyed the closed bedroom door, grabbed his keys and headed out. Fresh air and distance was what he needed. And he could check out the state of the roads while he was at it.

Ben took the drive into the village slowly. The snow showed no sign of melting, but the roads were clearer than he'd expected—obviously some of the local farm vehicles had already been out. Ben parked up outside the Eight Bells and decided he deserved a warming cup of some-thing, and maybe some of Tracy's homemade cake, before he hit the village store for supplies and a weather forecast.

Johnny, the landlord, raised his eyebrows from behind the pumps at the sight of him. 'Didn't expect to see you out of bed so early.'

'It's gone ten,' Ben pointed out, leaning against the bar.

'Exactly.' Johnny reached behind him to flick the cof-fee machine on. 'Tracy said it looked like you and your new friend were planning to hit the sheets for the rest of the week when you left here last night.'

'Well, Tracy was wrong,' Ben said, trying not to think about how close to right she might have been. 'Besides, Luce is an old friend—not a new one. We were at univer-sity together.' No need to get into the details.

'Hmm.' The corners of Johnny's mouth dipped down for a moment, as if to say, *Okay, then. If you say so,* as he handed over a cup of coffee.

'What?'

'Just… You do realise she's the first person—male or female—you've ever brought to my pub?'

'So?'

'Is she the first person you've taken up to your cottage at all?'

An uncomfortable feeling crept up Ben's back. 'Yeah. We were driving to Cardiff when the snow got heavy, so we stopped off here.'

'That explains it, then, I guess. We just figured she must be someone important.' He didn't sound pleased at the explanation. 'So. Old friend?'

'Yeah, you know. Nice to catch up and stuff.' Ben picked up his coffee, and motioned to one of the tables by the window. 'Anyway, I'd better drink up and get back to her. Lousy host, really.'

'I can imagine,' Johnny said.

But the frown line between his eyebrows told Ben he was still a little disappointed by the set-up.

*Why?* he wondered as he made his way over to the table. Was it so inconceivable that he'd bring a friend to visit? Just because he hadn't done it in the last few years? Why *hadn't* he, actually? He supposed it hadn't occurred to him. The women he spent time with all preferred a night at one of the hotels, the swankier the better, and since Hampton & Sons didn't have anything under five stars except their newest acquisitions—in this case, the Royal Court, which had a measly four—it was easier just to check into the nearest one. And if he was meeting friends it was the local pub or the curry house. No need for them to trek all the way to the middle of nowhere in Wales. Besides, the cottage was *his* place. It was where he went when he needed to escape from the real world. There'd never been much point in bringing the real world with him.

Luce wasn't the real world. This brief sojourn in the

snow had nothing to do with reality. Once he'd taken her back to Cardiff the brief time bubble would be over and he'd forget all about her for another eight years, while he got on with his life and she refused to. Easy.

His phone rang as soon as he sat down. 'Hampton.'

'Other Hampton.'

Seb's dry voice sounded out of place as Ben sat staring across at the Welsh mountains. Seb was urban and urbane. He was the city, and the company, and the polished wood of his office.

He'd definitely never invited Seb up to the cottage. Maybe he should.

'What can I do for you today, oh, fearless leader?'

'Stop calling me that, for a start.'

On the other end of the line Ben heard his brother shuffling papers before he continued.

'I just got through reading your report from Chester.'

'And?'

A pause. Never good.

Then Seb said, 'When are you back in London?'

'Tomorrow night was the plan. Might make it Friday— snow dependent.'

'Can you stop by and see me on Friday? I know it's Christmas Eve, and you're supposed to be off the rest of the week…'

'I can,' Ben said. 'But if there's a problem with my report I'd rather you just tell me now.'

Another pause.

'It's not a problem, exactly.'

Seb didn't sound annoyed, or let down, which Ben was pretty sure their father would have done. That was something.

'Just an idea I want to talk through with you.'

Now, *that* was new. For the last six months Seb had

been making the decisions and Ben had been making them happen. That was how they operated, and it worked well. But if Seb was willing to let him in, loosen his grip on the reins… *Maybe he won't turn into Dad after all.*

'Okay. So, how's London coping without me?'

'Never mind London,' Seb said. 'Tell me about this brunette from Chester. Did you actually take her to your cottage? The forbidden inner sanctum?'

It felt wrong to hear Luce described that way, and Ben regretted ever mentioning her to Seb. He clamped down on the surge of anger filling his chest, reminding himself that Seb was only talking about her the way Ben himself had, last time they'd spoken.

'It's not… She's an old friend,' Ben said, repeating the line he'd used with Johnny and wondering why it felt like such a lie. Because they'd never really *been* friends, he supposed. 'I was driving her back to Cardiff and we detoured to the cottage because of the snow.'

'Wow. You *did* actually take her to your fabled cottage? I was kidding about that part. She must be pretty important.'

'More that I didn't want to die in a snowy crash,' Ben assured him. 'Her train was cancelled, I was headed this way anyway, so I drove her. That's all.'

'Hmm.'

Ben didn't think Seb needed to sound quite so disbelieving. 'Yeah, well, I should get back to my host duties,' he said, draining his coffee. 'I'll see you on Friday.'

It didn't matter what Seb thought about Luce, he reminded himself as he stood and put on his coat. Because after today she'd be out of his life again.

Which was a good thing. Right?

Except if he wasn't going to see her again… The thought of not having her, just once, burned at his heart.

He needed to touch her, to feel her—hell, even just to hold her. The memory of her swaying into his arms the night before wasn't fading. How could he *not* experience more than that?

But after turning her down the night before...? Ben wasn't stupid. She wasn't going to ask again. He'd head back to the cottage, they'd pack up the car and drive to Cardiff, and that would be it. He'd blown the only chance he'd get with Luce Myles.

But as he left the Eight Bells a leaflet in the rack for tourists caught his eye, and Ben realised that maybe there was one more thing he could give Luce before they parted ways. Something for her to remember these strange, snowy few days by.

Pocketing the leaflet, he headed over to the village shop, his mood suddenly a whole lot lighter.

It hadn't been Luce's most productive morning ever.

She'd started well—up with the lark and at the desk with her computer cursor blinking at her. Outside, the snow looked as if it might be starting to clear, which gave her hope that they might make it to Cardiff today. She'd heard the front door slam after she'd been working a couple of hours, and reasoned that Ben had probably gone to check on the conditions. She'd have to wait until he got back to face him. Heat had flooded to her cheeks at the very thought. Really no hurry on that one. Then they'd be on their way and it would all be over. She'd be home again.

In the meantime, the book wouldn't write itself.

The first couple of pages of the section dealing with Nest's life at Cilgerran Castle, before her abduction, had come in an inspired burst, leaving her feeling buoyant and excited. And then...nothing.

After another half an hour of staring at the screen and

adjusting punctuation, Luce had given up and indulged in a long soak in the bath instead. Hot water and bubbles were almost guaranteed to help inspiration strike, surely?

Except when she settled back down at the desk, fully dressed in a long knitted skirt and wine-red sweater, she still had nothing.

'Going well?'

Luce spun round to see Ben leaning against the door-frame, arms folded over his chest and his eyebrow raised. He betrayed no sign of his rejection the night before—which was a small point in his favour, Luce supposed.

'I think I'm getting some really useful stuff,' she lied, and hoped he hadn't heard the bath water draining out.

Ben held up a bakery bag. 'Well, brunch will help. I brought ham and cheese croissants.'

Luce's stomach rumbled at the very mention.

As they sat down together at the small kitchen table Luce asked, 'What are the roads like? Can we make Cardiff today?'

Ben nodded, already chewing. 'More snow due tonight, but we should be able to beat it.'

She should be relieved. Thrilled that she was heading home. So what was with the strange, sad part of her that was already missing the cottage before they'd even left?

And not just the cottage. The company.

Luce stared down at her plate. Definitely time to go.

'I should go and get packed up, then,' she said, even though the only things she'd really unpacked were her laptop and notes.

'Actually...'

Ben paused and she looked up at him. Was he going to ask her to stay? No. That was ridiculous.

'There's somewhere I'd like to take you. Before you go. It's not exactly on our way, but I think it'll be worth it.'

Luce frowned. 'How out of our way? Where is it?'

'It's a surprise.' Ben's smile was slow and teasing. 'But I promise you you'll like it.'

The problem with that, Luce reflected, was that what she liked and wanted wasn't always good for her. But if this was her last ever day with Ben, how could she turn down the chance to spend a few more hours with him?

'Finish your croissant first,' he said, and she obeyed.

Twenty minutes later they were all packed up. Pulling on her thick coat and boots, Luce followed Ben out to the car, her eyes drawn to the way his upper body filled out his coat. He really had grown into his size over the last eight years. How was she supposed to forget how good it had felt to be held against that chest the night before when he was just *there*, looking gorgeous?

Of course after today he wouldn't be.

Sighing, she got into the car, fastening her seatbelt without looking at him again. Instead, she looked back at the cottage as they drove away, and wondered if there was any chance she'd ever see it again.

'You okay?' Ben asked as they reached the main road out of the village.

'Fine.' She flashed him a quick smile, then glanced away. So much pretty countryside to look at, all white and sparkling. Why should she look at him anyway? 'Are you really not going to tell me where we're going?'

'I told you. It's a surprise.'

Luce didn't know the area well enough to be able to guess where they were headed, and by the time they hit the bigger roads she was too absorbed in her own thoughts and the snow-capped hills and frosted trees around her to pay attention to road signs. What would this countryside have looked like in Nest's time? Would she have ridden through these hills? How had it felt when she'd had to leave this landscape behind and move to England?

What would Ben do if she kissed him?

Luce closed her eyes. *No.* Back to what mattered. Nest. Her book. Not her sex drive.

Although Nest had obviously had enough of one, given the number of men she'd been connected to and the number of children she'd borne.

Not the point. Okay. Enough about Nest the woman. Focus on the book itself. The structure. Should she break Chapter Seven into two parts? Should she ask Ben in for dinner when they got to Cardiff? Or more...

Oh, God, this was hopeless.

'We're here,' Ben said, his voice amused, and Luce realised belatedly that the car had stopped moving.

Fumbling with the handle, Luce threw the door open and stepped out into the snow. She smoothed down her skirt with one hand, aware that Ben was walking around the car towards her.

'Figured out where we are yet?' he asked.

He was standing too close for her to think straight. She could feel the warmth of his breath on her neck, a wonderful contrast to the wintry chill.

She stepped away quickly and looked up. 'Oh!'

The twin round towers of Cilgerran Castle loomed overhead, grey and dark against the sky, snow capping them, and Luce's breath caught in her throat. She'd have known where she was in an instant, even without the information board at the edge of the car park. This place mattered. This was history made real, right before her. 'This is it. This is—'

'Cilgerran Castle. Where they say Nest was abducted from.'

Ben moved behind her and she could feel his warmth through her coat.

'Good idea?'

She nodded, her head jerking up and down hard to show him just what a fantastic idea she thought it was. This was what she needed. To get close to Nest physically as well as intellectually. She needed to stand where she had stood, needed to feel the stone walls around her. Needed to understand how Nest had felt so many years ago.

Why hadn't she come here before? Oh, she had, she supposed, back when she was studying for her Masters and Nest had been just a passing interest in half a module of her course. But never since. After all, she'd done it already. Why waste the day getting there and back to Cardiff again when there was so much else she needed to do?

But she'd never felt then what she felt now. The feeling that all of history was coming together in one place, just to help her understand.

'I hadn't realised it was so close,' she murmured, and felt Ben shrug behind her. He was so close, too.

'A couple of hours. You were daydreaming on the way here.'

Had it really been that long? They could have got to Cardiff and back already. 'I was thinking about Nest.' Mostly.

'I saw a leaflet for it in the Eight Bells rack earlier. Thought it looked like your sort of thing. And when I remembered how you told me Nest had lived here, was taken from here, I had to bring you.'

Luce spun round, finding herself nose to chest with him. How had she forgotten he was so close? His hand settled on her waist to steady her when she stumbled on the uneven ground and heat radiated through Luce's body. Raising her gaze to meet his, she said, 'Thank you.'

'You're welcome.'

The words were simple, but the emotions they evoked were anything but. His lips were just inches away. If she went up on tiptoes she could kiss him so easily. It would be a thank-you kiss, nothing more, but she'd get to feel his mouth against hers. And, oh, how she wanted to...

She bit down on her own lip to try to curb the temptation. But Ben's fingers still pressed against her waist. Then he glanced away, hands dropping from her body, and she saw his Adam's apple bob as he swallowed.

'Shall we go in?' he asked.

Luce stepped back and nodded again. Nest—that was why she was here. And then she was leaving. She really had to try to remember that.

# CHAPTER TEN

BEN WATCHED LUCE's rear move enticingly under that touchable flowing skirt as she gripped the handrail of the bridge over the moat, struggling to keep her footing on the icy wood as she made her way into the castle. It had seemed like such a good, obvious idea to bring her when he'd seen the leaflet. Killing two birds with one big hunk of tumbledown rock. Lots of Brownie points for him for thinking of it, meaning she'd be thinking kindly of him again as they drove to Cardiff. Maybe even enough to say yes if he asked her to dinner again. He could spend the night in Cardiff, head straight to London in the morning. Because this wasn't over yet. It couldn't be.

Memories of his twenty-first birthday flashed through his mind again. He'd wanted to seduce this woman eight years ago, before he'd even really known her. And now that feeling was a thousand times stronger.

He was pretty sure she'd go along with it this time, if he did. Last night's awkward resolution notwithstanding, he'd seen the signs. The way her body swayed into his whenever he got close, the way her eyes widened when her gaze caught his. And the way her teeth had pressed down into her lip, displaying just how plump and kissable it was. Her resistance was definitely crumbling.

He had to stop thinking about this. He had to wait. Otherwise he'd be seducing her up against a very cold stone castle keep.

Inside the castle walls Ben found a bench near an information board, brushed off the snow as best he could and sat down to watch the show. Cilgerran was a nice enough castle, he supposed, but not exactly his main area of interest. That, right now, would be Luce.

The castle had free entry until the end of March, but no one else was taking advantage of it. Clearly the weather had scared them off, but they were missing out, Ben thought. Luce flitted from wall to wall, from snow-covered step to window, from arch to arrow-hole, the breeze keeping her skirt plastered against her curves under her short jacket, her colour high and eyes bright. From time to time she'd call out to him, telling him about what she was looking at, what had happened here. The wind whisked away every other word, but it didn't matter. Ben didn't care about the castle. He was too entranced by her.

She was beautiful.

It wasn't as if he hadn't noticed before, of course. But it had always been a pale, reserved beauty. The sort you could look at but not touch. Hell, she'd practically had 'Keep Out' signs plastered all over her. But here...here she was radiant. She was real. And how he wanted to touch her.

He couldn't have said how long it was before she jumped down from the low remains of an interior wall, sending a puff of snow flying up. Time seemed to pass differently when he was absorbed in watching her.

Her cheeks were pink and flushed as she flung herself onto the patch of bench he'd cleared beside him. 'This place is fantastic,' she said, sounding slightly out of breath from hopping around the castle walls.

'I'm glad you like it.' The urge to lean back against the bench, stretch an arm around her shoulders and pull her

into him was almost overpowering. In an attempt to resist, Ben leant forward instead, resting his forearms along
his thighs. 'It must have been pretty impressive back in
the day.'

'It's impressive now.'

Luce's voice held a tone of reverence, and he knew she
saw something here that he never could—something beyond his world. It didn't matter. He was content to enjoy
it through her, to see her eyes light up at the history she
saw here. He'd bring her back every week if he could. Just
to see that sparkle, that life in her face.

Except maybe it would wear off over time. Maybe they'd
have to tour all the castles in Wales. And the rest of Britain. And overseas. *I wonder how she feels about French
châteaux?*

Or maybe he'd take her back to Cardiff and never see
her again, as planned.

That thought made the winter air colder, the clouds
overhead more threatening. Ben squinted up at the sky.
The reports said no more snow until that night, but those
skies just screamed bad weather. They should get going
or they might not make it to Cardiff. Again.

But he didn't want to leave. Not yet. He wanted a little more time with this Luce first. Excited, vibrant, castle
Luce. Was that so much to ask?

'So, where do you think Nest was taken from?' Ben
got to his feet as he spoke, reaching a hand out to pull
Luce up again.

She rolled her eyes as she stood. 'The castle would
have looked completely different then. Most of what you
see today was probably built in the thirteenth century—a
hundred years or more after Owain took Nest.'

'Okay, so tell me what it would have looked like then.'

'Earth and timber building, probably. We can't really

be sure.' Luce gazed around her again and Ben realised he was staring at her the same way she looked at the castle. He didn't stop.

Luce carried on talking, almost as if to herself. 'It doesn't matter that it looks different now. The landscape's the same. The feeling. She was here, and now I am. And I feel... It's ridiculous.' She dropped her head.

'Go on,' Ben said, trying to resist the desperate temptation to move closer to her.

Luce reached out to place a hand against the stone of the castle wall, palm flat, as if she were connecting herself to the site. 'I feel like I can understand her better here. Make more sense of her life and what happened to her. There's so few facts that we can be sure about. But here they come together better.'

'So it's helped?'

She looked up, her eyes wide and shining, and smiled at him. Ben felt the moment he lost himself as a dull ache in his chest.

'It's helped a lot,' she said. 'Thank you.'

It was too late, now, he realised. He'd been hers since the moment he saw her again in Chester. Maybe longer. Maybe since that night in the library. It didn't matter. None of it mattered any more. He just had to have her.

Stepping forward, he raised his hands to her cold face, his body moving into her space as she fell back to rest against the castle wall.

'We should get going.'

Sharp white teeth bit down on her lip again after she spoke, and Ben almost groaned at the sight.

'I know.' But he didn't move away.

'Kiss me,' she said, anyway, and he lowered his mouth to hers, the wind whipping round them, cold and icy and utterly unimportant in the moment.

Her lips were soft and sweet under his as he teased them open, drinking in the taste and the feel of her. Luce's arms wrapped around his waist, her hands firm against his back, pulling him in deeper, closer, even as he pressed his body against hers, the softness of her curves driving him wild.

As the first cold drops hit the back of his neck, Ben pulled his mouth away, his hands tugging her body into the warmth and safety of his arms. Luce rubbed her cheek against his coat and he kissed the top of her head.

'We need to get out of here,' he said, and she moved away, leaving him cold and bereft.

She blinked up at him and snowflakes landed on her lashes. 'It's snowing again.'

'And it's going to get heavier. But, more importantly, I need to get you somewhere more private than a ruined public castle.' He took a breath. 'So—Cardiff or the cottage?'

Luce's lips quirked up in a naughty smile, and the expression was so utterly unexpected that Ben bit back a laugh.

'Whichever is closer,' she said, and he grabbed her hand as they ran for the exit.

*Finally,* Ben thought, as the car doors slammed behind them and he set a course back to the cottage. Finally something was looking up.

The journey back to the cottage seemed to take twice as long as the trip to the castle had done, and that was only due in part to the increasingly heavy snowfall. It seemed worse even than the drive from Chester had been. Cardiff would have to wait another day, apparently, but somehow the thought bothered her far less now. She couldn't have left without having this, having *him*, just once.

Ben drove steadily through the worsening weather, taking bends and dips in his stride. Luce kept her hands clenched against her knees, more to stop herself touching him than from fear of the drive.

'You okay?' he asked finally, just as the sky went from grey to black and Luce made out a sign welcoming them to the Brecon Beacons National Park through the falling snow.

'I'm fine,' she said.

'Really?'

*No. I want you to pull over so I can ravish you in the back seat.* Luce felt her eyes widen at the very thought. Not a very Dr Lucinda Myles type desire at all.

'You're not over-thinking this?'

She looked up at Ben as he spoke. His eyes were still firmly on the road, his arms braced tight to the wheel. He looked as if every muscle in his body was taut. Was that because of the weather? Or because he was resisting a similar urge to hers?

Luce gave herself one moment to believe it was the latter, then realised she still hadn't answered his question. With a soft laugh she said, 'Honestly, Ben, I'm barely thinking at all right now.'

She was watching, so she saw him blow out a long breath, saw his shoulders sink, his body start to relax. Had he really been that worried about her?

'I'm not going to fall apart because you kissed me, you know,' she said, forehead furrowed with the effort of trying to figure out what he was thinking.

His mouth slipped into a half-smile. 'Yeah, but I might if I don't get to do it again soon.'

The heat that pooled in her belly seemed hotter, more desperate at his words than it had been even in the castle. Back there she'd told herself it was the location, the romanticism of the castle and its history. But here, when he should be focused on the road, he was still thinking about kissing her.

'Are we nearly there yet?' She could hear the wanting in her own voice, and Ben obviously did, too. He glanced over at her, just for a moment, surprise on his face.

'Nearly,' he answered, his voice low and full of promise.

Luce was almost certain that the rest of the journey took considerably less time than it should have done. But he had to slow down again as they reached the twisting path up to the cottage itself, and Luce gripped the edge of her seat as the car slipped and slid over the still falling snow. *Not going to be fun trying to get back through this to Cardiff, even tomorrow.*

The thought was too depressing to dwell on. Instead, Luce focused on thinking about what might happen when they got inside the cottage and bit her lip.

'Okay, this is as close as we're getting,' Ben said eventually, wrestling the car onto the side of the road and pulling on the handbrake. They hadn't even made it to the parking spot they'd managed the day before. This snowstorm was making yesterday's look like a mere sprinkling. 'Think you can walk from here?'

Luce nodded because, honestly, she could do anything if it meant Ben was going to kiss her again soon.

He trudged round to the other side of the car, helping her out into the snow, and pulled her arm through his so he held her tight against the side of his body. Together, heads down against the snow flurries, they made their slow way up the last of the hill to the cottage, with Ben yanking her upright whenever her boots slipped.

And then, just when Luce had started to fear they were never going to make it, the cottage appeared through the snow, and warmth burst through her despite the weather.

Ben fumbled the door open and in moments had slammed

it shut behind them and pressed her up against it, his hands cold as they found their way under her coat and jumper to bare skin. His lips were hot, though, warm and demanding, and Luce let her head fall back against the wood and surrendered herself to his kiss.

Then he wrenched himself away again and Luce's body ached with the loss.

'This is what you want?' he asked.

Luce nodded furiously. 'Of course—'

'For *you*,' he interrupted. His eyes were dark with want, but his face was serious. 'Not because someone else wants you to, or because it's what you should do, or even because you're trying to be something you weren't in university. Because you want it.'

'Yes.'

'And you know…you know what this is?'

At last Luce realised what he really wanted, and even though she'd promised herself she wouldn't give it to him, the need that burned through her body meant she couldn't stop the words even if she wanted to.

'I want you, Ben. Me. I want your hands and your mouth and your body on me. Just for tonight. Just one night.'

His hands tightened around her waist as she spoke and Luce swallowed at the heat in his eyes. Then she said the words she knew he was waiting for.

'Seduce me.'

That was all Ben needed to hear. With a growl of satisfaction he captured her lips again, even as his hands pushed her coat from her shoulders.

'You're wearing far too many clothes,' he murmured, working his kisses down her throat.

She bent her neck enticingly, to give him better access, and he allowed himself a moment to admire the pale skin there, and the line of her throat to her shoulders. How had he never noticed how beautiful she was when they were younger? Maybe she was more confident now, better dressed, more aware of her own attraction. But her beauty had always lain in the essence of her, the bones and the lines, and he just hadn't been looking carefully enough.

Except for that one night, drunk and stupid. Then he'd seen it.

'It was cold in the castle,' Luce said, and Ben had to concentrate to remember what they'd even been talking about. He was past words already.

God, how had she bewitched him so completely, so quickly? Taken charge of his senses so that all that mattered was getting her in his bed as quickly as possible? Hell, he didn't even care about the bed. He was on the verge of taking her right here against the door.

He needed to regain some control. He needed to be able to walk away from this tomorrow. The wild, blood-boiling feeling that had taken over had stripped away what he knew of himself. He needed this to be back on his terms.

With more effort than he would have liked, he pulled her away from the door. 'Bedroom,' he said, sentences still beyond him.

Luce glanced around as though she'd forgotten entirely where she was, hadn't even noticed the splintered door at her back. At least he wasn't the only one losing control.

She followed him without argument as he tugged her towards his bedroom and kicked the door shut behind them. He'd worried that she might be spooked when they were finally there, that once it became too real she'd change her mind. But instead she melted into his arms as he stripped off her clothes, her fingers already dragging his jumper up over his head.

Skin to skin, touch to touch, Ben laid her back on the

bed, covering her with his own body. She was so smooth under his hands, and every touch made her arch and moan and mew, responsive in a way he could never have imagined. And he responded in turn, his fingers and his mouth reaching deeper, more demanding, until finally, *finally*, he slid home into her and felt her moan against his shoulder.

'Okay?' He kissed her ear as they stilled for a moment, letting her adjust.

'More than,' she whispered back, and then Ben couldn't help but move and move, until she was falling apart under him, and his whole world narrowed to the feel of her, to a pinpoint of sensation that made his body tense until it might break...

Afterwards, once enough of his brain had returned to his body, Ben rolled onto his side, pulling Luce with him so she was tucked safe in his arms. Her breathing was the only sound, deep and even, as if she were trying to bring her body back under her own control. It was too late, though. He'd already seen the wildness at the centre of her, the free parts she kept locked up tight. The hidden side of her that wanted, wanted—wanted so much.

He couldn't let her lock that up again.

# CHAPTER ELEVEN

THE ROOM LAY under a strange hush, as if nothing existed beyond the bed in which they lay. Luce supposed it was the snow, blanketing the world outside and deadening the sounds. But maybe it was the sex as well. After all, such a moment deserved a reverential silence, surely?

Because it wasn't just sex. Luce felt a stab in her chest at the realisation, and she must have flinched, because Ben's arm tightened around her, pulling her closer into that magnificent chest. She felt his mouth brush against her hair, soothing, comforting. As if he was trying not to startle her.

'Freaking out?' he asked, his voice a murmur. But the grip on her body told her he wasn't letting go even if she was.

'A little,' she admitted, and cursed herself even as she spoke. The last thing she needed Ben to know was that sex had reduced her to a gibbering wreck.

Except it wasn't the sex. The sex had been phenomenal, taking her everywhere she'd needed to go and then some. Her whole body was thanking her for the sex in its own languid, melted way. No, the sex was just fine.

It was the feelings that went along with it that caused the problems.

She wasn't deluded enough to think that Ben would break his one-night rule for her. But, lying in his arms, it was hard to imagine how she would tear herself away the next morning.

But she had to. Because Ben wasn't a man looking for responsibility, family, a wife. And she knew herself. She wasn't Nest, for all that she'd been taken from Cilgerran Castle and bedded tonight. She had a family she had to take care of, and Ben would never be able to bear to have anything take affections away from him. If she were to fall in love, to find someone to make a life with, it had to be someone who supported her, helped her, understood that she had other responsibilities.

Ben Hampton was not that man. Ben was so far from being that man it was almost funny. Or hugely depressing.

The best she could hope for with Ben was an occasional night together when he happened to be in town and it suited him—and even then never more than one night in a row. And that wasn't enough for her. He wanted her to think about her own needs? Well, she needed more than that from a relationship.

'What can I do to help you relax?' he asked, his voice soft and seductive.

Luce felt her body reacting even though every muscle in it was already exhausted.

'I'm never going to be able to sleep if you keep thinking so loud. Normally a woman is more relaxed after I finish my work.' He sounded faintly put out at that.

Luce bit her lip. She had to leave tomorrow morning. She knew that. But that didn't mean she couldn't make the most of her one night.

Shifting in his arms so she was facing him, Luce let him pull her flush against him, her breasts brushing against the hairs on his chest, his right leg pressing between her thighs.

'Maybe you haven't finished work for the night, then,' she said, and watched his eyes darken as he smiled.

Yes, if she only got one night with Ben Hampton, Luce was going to make sure every moment counted.

According to the clock on the bedside table, it was late morning when Ben awoke, but the room remained dim and close. *Guess it hasn't stopped snowing, then.* He supposed he could get up and look, see what they were dealing with. But the bed was so warm, and when he shifted Luce snuggled closer into his arms.

Yeah, he wasn't going anywhere in a hurry.

And neither, he realised, was she. Not if the snow was as heavy as it had looked before they'd retired to the bedroom for the night. If he hadn't been able to get the car all the way up to the cottage yesterday afternoon, they'd be lucky even to get back to it this morning. No point even trying.

Not, of course, that logic meant she wouldn't need some convincing of that fact. Ben smiled. Given how responsive she'd been to his 'convincing' the night before, he didn't see it being a particularly arduous task.

'Are you awake?' Luce asked, her voice fuzzy with sleep.

'Yeah,' he murmured, and she turned over in his arms to face him.

'Has it stopped snowing?'

She was blinking up at him, her hair falling into her eyes, her face pink and sleepy, and Ben thought she looked more beautiful than he'd ever seen her.

'Don't know.'

Wriggling out of his embrace, she wrapped the extra blanket from the bottom of the bed around her and padded to the window, ducking under the curtain to look out.

Then she swore. Ben didn't think he'd ever heard her do that before. He hadn't even been sure she knew such words.

Flinging the curtains open, she turned to him with an

accusing glare. 'Look at it! It's piled up halfway to the window! We're never going to get back to Cardiff in this!'

Shuffling into a seated position, lounging against the headboard, Ben shrugged. 'So we spend another day here. Is that so bad?'

'Yes!' Luce ran a hand through her tangled hair and almost lost her grip on the blanket. 'It's Christmas Eve *tomorrow*, Ben. I have to get home. Never mind the book. I've got to get things ready for my family. I haven't even *thought* about dinner for tomorrow.' She yanked the blanket up again, covering all but a hint of her cleavage. 'This is all your fault.'

'I thought we'd established that I can't control the weather?' Ben said mildly.

'Maybe not. But you said it wouldn't snow again until last night. And you didn't tell me it would be heavy enough to drift!'

Ben winced. That much was, in fact, true. He'd known how bad the snow would be and still brought her back here, instead of taking her home. 'I gave you a choice: the cottage or Cardiff. You chose here.'

'Because I didn't have all the information! You *trapped* me here.'

She looked so anguished Ben almost felt sorry for her. Except that she was trying to blame him for her decisions and accusing him of imaginary plots. Again. As if he hadn't done all he could to help her for the last three days. As if what they'd shared was nothing more than an attempt to get her into bed. Well, if that was what she thought— fine. Let her believe him to be exactly the sort of man she'd always thought. She'd never believe he'd changed, anyway. So why should he change? What had he been thinking to believe for even a moment that this could be

more than a one-night stand? They were as different now
as they'd ever been.

'Trapped you here?' Ben raised his eyebrows in de-
liberate disbelief. 'Why would I do that? You know my
one-night rule. Trust me—I'm as ready to get back to ci-
vilisation as you are.'

He wished he could take back the words the moment
he'd spoken them. Not least because he knew he'd put an
end to any chance of spending another day—and night—
in bed with Luce. But mostly because of the way her face
froze, eyes wide, mouth slightly open, fingers wrapped in
the blanket as she held it tight to her chest.

The moment lasted too long—a cold chill between them
as the silence of the snow pressed in. Then Luce broke. She
took a step back, towards the door, and shook her head just
a little. 'Of course. If we're stuck here I need to work. Tell
me when it clears enough for us to leave.'

She didn't even slam the door behind her. Instead she
closed it carefully, letting the latch click quietly into place.
And Ben fell back down onto the bed and wished he'd
never heard of Cilgerran Castle.

Luce fumbled her way into her clothes with chilly fingers,
trying to convince herself that it was only the cold making her shake. But the anger still bubbling up in her chest
told her different.

She was furious. With Ben, naturally, for being exactly
what she'd always known he was. And she was even more
angry with herself.

Dropping to sit on the bed as she yanked on thick socks
over her woolly tights, Luce tried to calm down. She'd
never get any work done like this.

How could she have been so stupid? She knew beyond
a doubt exactly what sort of a man Ben was. Hell, he'd told

her himself! His ridiculous one-night rule was a prime example. As if only spending one night together could make falling in love less likely.

Not that she was in love with Ben Hampton. Not even *she* was that idiotic.

She'd brought this on herself. *Take responsibility. Take control.* Well, she'd take the responsibility, anyway. Control seemed to be entirely out of her hands.

This was her punishment for taking what she wanted for a change—for forgetting about her obligations, about her family. Would the snow clear for them to get through? The thought of spending another night in the cottage, even in her own room, made her shiver. And what if she didn't make it home for Christmas Eve and Tom's dinner? Or, worse, Christmas Day itself?

If giving in to her foolish desire to sleep with Ben Hampton ruined Christmas for her family they'd never forgive her. Hell, she'd never forgive herself.

In a flurry of movement Luce crossed the room and settled into the chair, flipping open her laptop and tapping her fingers against the wood of the desk as she waited for it to bring up her manuscript. Work. That was what she needed. Something to distract her and give her purpose. Except...

*How am I supposed to concentrate on ancient history when my own past and present is naked in the next room?*

No, she needed to focus. Nest. What happened after Owain took her from Cilgerran? Henry I intervened. So, how to frame it? Consider how one woman, a Welsh princess, caused uproar in the English court? Or tell the more personal story of her ex-lover coming to the rescue of her reputation?

Her lips tightened. God only knew what her grandfather would make of *her* reputation right now if he were still alive.

*Nest had it easy. One quick kidnapping and she was set.*

With a sigh, Luce turned her attention to the document in front of her and pushed all thoughts of Ben, the night before and what the hell happened next out of her head. The only thing she could fix right now was her book.

Ben was still cursing himself for an idiot two hours later when, as he waited for the kettle to boil for an apologetic cup of peppermint tea, the lights went out. Cursing, he flipped a few switches on and off, then stalked off towards the fuse box. Chances were it was a power cut, given the snow, but his luck had to turn some time. Maybe it was a tripped switch.

It wasn't. And by the time he returned to the kitchen Luce stood in front of the fire, arms crossed over her chest, glaring at him. 'What the hell's happened *now*?'

'Power cut,' Ben said. 'At least best I can tell. Might be a line down somewhere.'

'So what do we do?' Luce asked, a snap in her voice. 'Don't you have an emergency generator or something?'

At least she was talking to him. He supposed he should be grateful for that. 'No generator. Now we build up the fire, keep warm and survive on whatever in the fridge doesn't need cooking.' Maybe he had some marshmallows they could toast somewhere at the back of a cupboard.

Luce glared out of the window and he followed her gaze to where the snow was still fluttering to the ground. 'I'm thinking very fondly of the Eight Bells right now.'

'We'd never get down the path,' Ben said.

'Just as long as it clears enough for us to get to Cardiff. I'm not staying another day here with you.' Luce's tone was firm, as if daring the weather to disagree with her again. But, given the way the snow had started to drift, driving anywhere in the next few days would be a really stupid idea.

Of course getting snowed in at his cottage, during a power cut, with a furious Lucinda Myles was also kind of idiotic. Apparently there was something about her that made him lose his mind.

'Are you hungry?' he asked, checking his watch in the firelight. He wasn't sure what meal they were on, but it had been a while since either of them had eaten.

'That depends on what's in your fridge.' Luce eyed him with suspicion, as if he might be about to add poisoning to his list of crimes.

'I picked up some bits from the village shop yesterday. There should be enough to tide us over.' Just about. He'd only planned on having to feed himself, after all.

'Fine. But the power had better come back on before my laptop battery runs out.' Turning on her heel, Luce stalked back towards her room. 'Call me when the food's ready.'

Ben sighed and watched her go. Apparently any sort of reconciliation was still a way off.

There wasn't much to prepare. Ben arranged cheeses and bread on plates, adding some cold meats he'd picked up, then carried them over to the low table in front of the fire. Then, as an afterthought, he grabbed a bottle of red wine and two glasses. Wine always made things more of a feast.

'Grub's up,' he called, and moments later Luce appeared. She'd added another jumper on top of her outfit from earlier. With the electric under-floor heating out of commission the cottage was becoming very chilly, very quickly. 'Sorry it's not much.'

Luce took the glass of wine he'd poured for her and sat at the end of the sofa nearest the fire. 'Better than nothing.

At least it's warm in here.' Her words were short, terse. And she still wasn't looking at him.

With a deep breath, Ben sat down beside her, reaching for his own wine. 'That's not all I'm sorry for.'

Slowly she turned to look at him, without speaking. It wasn't much, but Ben took it as a sign she was at least willing to listen. 'I'm sorry about what I said. About...'

'Your one-night rule?'

'Yeah.'

'Fine.'

She'd turned her attention back to her plate again, picking at the bread. Ben watched her, waiting for something more, but it wasn't forthcoming.

'Not feeling inclined to apologise for accusing me of trapping you in this cottage purely to seduce you?'

'Not really.' She reached for her wine glass. 'Apart from anything else, you *did* seduce me.'

She had a point there. And somehow Ben knew that saying, *You asked me to* wasn't going to make anything any better.

'How does it even work, anyway?' she asked, after a long moment's silence in the flickering firelight. 'Your stupid rule? What? You just live your life going from one-night stand to one-night stand?'

'No.' Ben rubbed a hand across his forehead. *Now* she wanted to talk about this? There was a reason he usually had this talk before he hit the sheets. 'Of course not.'

'Then what?' Putting down her plate, Luce turned her body to face his, all attention on him. 'Come on. I want to know.'

For a moment she thought he wasn't going to answer. But, Luce rationalised, as a victim of his stupid rule, at the very least she deserved to understand it.

Finally Ben spoke. 'I date women. Same as anyone. I just make a point not to spend more than one night with them at a time.'

'Because twenty-four hours is too much like commit-ment?' Luce said, rolling her eyes. Men. What were they so damn scared of?

Ben sighed. 'Because if one night becomes two nights then it's all too easy for it to be three nights. A week. A month. More. And suddenly she's expecting a ring and a life. Something I can't give her.'

'You've tried, then?' Luce folded her legs up under her, twisting so her feet were closer to the hearth. With just the flickering fire to light the room it felt smaller, cosier. As if the world were only just big enough to encircle the two of them and their shadows.

'I don't have to. I've seen it before.' The way he said it, Luce knew that whatever he'd witnessed it had been up close and far too personal.

Frowning, she made an educated guess. 'Your parents?'

'Yeah.' Ben topped up their wine glasses, even though neither of them had drunk very much. 'Dad...his life was the business. Everything came second to Hampton & Sons. Even the sons.'

How must that have felt? Knowing he was less impor-tant than a building? Luce couldn't imagine. Her family might expect a lot from her, but at least she always knew they needed her.

'And your mum?' she asked.

Ben blew out a long breath. 'Mum would follow him around from business opportunity to networking dinner, smiling when he wanted her to smile, wearing what he wanted her to wear. She gave up her whole life to satisfy him, until finally she realised she'd given up herself.'

'She left?'

'When I was eight.' Ben stared into the fire. 'She just...
she couldn't do it any more. We didn't see her much after
that. And then she died two years later.'

Luce swallowed, her heart heavy in her chest. 'I'm
sorry. I never knew.' She could almost imagine him, ten
years old, perfectly turned out in a suit at his mother's
graveside. His heart must have broken. Was that when
he'd given up on family?

Ben shrugged. 'No reason you should. Anyway, that's
why. My life—it's all about fixing things and moving on.
Just like Dad. And I won't subject a wife or a child to that.'

'So you just don't let anyone get close enough to want
it?' Couldn't he see how bleak that existence was?

'Seems easiest.' He drained his wine and poured himself another glass. 'So, what about you? What is it that
makes *you* believe that bricks and mortar are important?
I mean, I'm all for lucrative property opportunities. But
your house is more than that to you, isn't it?'

'It's home,' Luce agreed. 'It always will be.'

'So tell me. What makes it home?'

Luce glanced over and saw that Ben's eyes were closed,
as if by not being able to see her he was distancing himself from the question he was asking. But if he wanted to
understand what made a house a home, she wasn't going
to deny him.

'It was my grandfather's house, originally. I told you
that, right?' She trailed her finger around the stem of her
glass, trying to find the words to explain what the house
meant to her. 'He bought it after he moved to Cardiff with
Grandma and made a little money, back in the fifties. It's
not in a great area, but it's still more than I could afford
to buy today. And it's close to the university.'

'He left it to you?'

Luce nodded. 'When he died, yeah. We grew up there,

you see. My father left when Dolly was a baby, and my Mum…that's when she retreated to her own bubble. Grandad moved us in, helped bring us up. Grandma had been dead for years, and the house was too big for just him, he always said.'

'You were his favourite, though,' Ben said. 'If he left you the house instead of your mum or your brother and sister.'

The unfairness of that act caught in Luce's chest every time she thought about it. 'It wasn't that, exactly. He relied on me to take care of them. The house needs a lot of work, and I don't think he thought they'd manage it. They all know it's still their home, too.'

'So you even give them your house?' Ben's eyes opened wide to stare at her. 'You really do give up everything for them, don't you?'

The cosy warmth of the fire started to cool and Luce pulled away a little. 'I don't expect you to understand,' she said, leaning back against the arm of the sofa.

Ben shrugged. 'Like I told you, home for me was hotels, after Mum left and Dad gave up the house. I used to think maybe I'd missed out, when I was a kid away at boarding school. But I like moving on—finding new things, new places.'

'But you bought this cottage,' Luce pointed out. 'You did it up, made it a home. You brought me here.'

She regretted the words as soon as they were spoken. She knew she shouldn't read more into that than a whim, an emergency pit stop in the snow. But it was so hard not to.

When she looked up his face was closed, his eyes staring over her head. 'The cottage is an investment. I'll probably sell it soon.'

The thought of Ben giving up his escape, the closest

thing he'd had to a home in years, without even realising what it meant, was too depressing to contemplate.

Looking away into the fire, she said, 'Doesn't look like the power's going to come back on tonight.'

'Yeah, I doubt it.' Ben gave her a look she couldn't quite read, then added, 'We'll have to see how the roads look in the morning.'

*No. No way.* Maybe she understood him a little better now, but that didn't mean she could stay here any longer and not go crazy. 'I'm sure they'll be fine.' Getting to her feet, she added, 'And a good night's sleep will do us both some good before the drive. I'll see you in the morning.'

She didn't look back, didn't check his expression, didn't wait for him to wish her goodnight. Even so, she barely made it to the door before the sound of his voice stopped her in her tracks.

'What if I said you were worth breaking my rule for?' he asked, so low she almost thought she must have misheard.

She turned back to face him, her heart thumping against her ribcage. 'But I'm not. I'm just the same Lucinda Myles you made fun of at university.'

Ben shook his head. 'You're so much more than I ever saw.'

Luce gave him a half-smile. 'So are you.'

And then, before she could change her mind, she shut the bedroom door behind her and climbed, fully clothed, into the freezing bed.

# CHAPTER TWELVE

BEN HAD PASSED a fitful night on the sofa, his dreams filled with dark hair and brick walls. But at least he'd been warm, he reasoned. Luce must have been half frozen in her lonely bed, if the way she'd appeared in front of the freshly banked fire before the sun had risen was any indication.

'Happy Christmas Eve,' she murmured as she held her hands out to the flames. Her suitcase leant beside the front door, just as it had in Chester, waiting to leave.

He sat up, blankets falling to his waist, and motioned at the case. 'You're still hoping to make it back to Cardiff today, then?'

'I have to.'

'To cook dinner for your family,' he said, a little disbelievingly.

'To spend Christmas with them,' she corrected. 'Don't you want to get back to London to spend it with your brother?'

'I think Seb wants me there for a business meeting rather than to sing carols round the piano.' Come to think of it, what *did* Seb want him there for? He'd been so preoccupied with Luce he'd barely given the strange conversation with his brother another thought.

'Fine. Maybe you don't care about family, or home, or Christmas. But I need to get back. Will you drive me?'

She looked down at him, eyes wide and dark, her hair curling around her face, and Ben knew he couldn't say no to her.

'If the roads are clear.' It wasn't a promise, but it felt like one all the same.

Luce nodded. 'I'll pack up the car.'

The roads weren't clear, not by anyone's definition. But the snow had stopped, and by lunchtime the tractors were out clearing some of the local thoroughfares. Once Ben had spent another hour digging his four-by-four out of the snow that had built up around it, and reversed onto the track, the journey looked manageable.

Still, it wasn't until they got out of the Brecon Beacons National Park and onto larger roads that Ben finally felt his shoulders start to relax as he settled into the drive. He'd driven through worse weather, especially up in the hills in France, by the château, but that didn't mean it was his preferred time to travel. Didn't mean he wasn't still annoyed with Luce for making him.

*That's why. That's the only reason. Nothing to do with her leaving me.*

Something he wasn't going to think about until this drive was over.

As they entered Cardiff Luce gave quiet, monotone directions to her house and Ben could feel his time with her slipping away. Being wasted. But what was the point? Her family would always be more important than him. And he would never be able to give her enough to make her stay. Neither one of them was going to change now, if they hadn't already. Why put himself through that?

Eventually he pulled up outside a row of townhouses, most of them converted into flats. Luce had the car door open almost before he'd switched the engine off, so he got out and went to open the boot for her.

'Want me to carry this in for you?' He hefted her suitcase out of the car and rested it on the pavement, his fingers still on the handle.

Luce shook her head. 'I can manage.'

And wasn't that her all over? 'Fine,' he said, relinquishing his hold.

She paused, biting down on her lip again, and Ben tried to ignore the heat that flooded through him at the sight.

'Thank you,' she said, finally. 'For this week.'

'I know it wasn't what you planned. But I hope you found the time away...useful.'

'I did, actually.' She sounded surprised.

'Good.'

What else was there left to say?

Awkward silence stretched between them until Luce motioned towards her front door and said, 'I'd better go and get ready.'

'The dinner party.' Ben nodded, his neck feeling stiff. 'Of course.'

'I know it doesn't seem like—'

'It's your life,' he interrupted, too tired to have the argument again. 'Do whatever you want, Luce.'

As he got back into the car he could have sworn he heard her say, 'That's the problem.' But by the time he turned round she'd already gone inside.

He thought about going straight back to the cottage, but he knew the memory of her would linger there. He'd call his usual cleaning lady, get her to clear the place out so that all reminders would be gone by his next visit.

He could check into a hotel, he supposed, if any had a spare room on Christmas Eve. But suddenly he wanted to see his brother. He wanted to know what Seb had planned next for the business. Something about this time with Luce had left him unsettled, unsure. And he needed something to throw himself into.

Decision made, he climbed back into the car and headed east, watching the snow that had disrupted his life thin and finally disappear as he sped along the M4.

He drove straight to Seb's office, figuring—correctly—that even late on Christmas Eve his brother would still be hard at work.

'You look terrible,' Seb said, as Ben sprawled in the visitor's chair on the opposite side of their dad's antique desk.

The usual unease and uncertainty rose up in Ben, just as it always had when Dad had been in residence behind the desk, but he clamped down on it, folded his ankle up on one knee and leant back, arms spread along the arms of the chair. Disrespectful and uncaring. Because Seb didn't need good posture to know he had his respect, and his dad wasn't there to care any more.

*Neither is Luce.*

'Hell of a drive in,' Ben said. 'Hills are practically snow-bound.'

Seb's eyebrows pulled down into a frown. 'This could have waited, you know. Until the weather cleared, at least.'

Ben shrugged. 'Needed to get back anyway.'

With a knowing look, Seb settled back in his chair. 'Ah. Time to let the latest girlfriend know she was only temporary, right? I'm just amazed you managed more than one night. Time to retire your rule at last?'

'No,' Ben said, shortly. 'The rule stays. And it's Christmas Eve. She had some family thing she had to get back for.'

Ben stared out of the window, trying to ignore the sense of wrongness that filled him when Seb talked about Luce as one of his girlfriends. Why did it feel so different?

Hadn't it followed the exact same pattern it always did? A bit of fun, discovering they were entirely different people, and then going their separate ways. Except this time they'd known just how different they were before they even went out to dinner. They'd wanted each other anyway.

Seb hadn't said anything, Ben realised. When he drew his attention back to his brother he found Seb watching him, a contemplative look in his eye.

'What?' Ben asked, shifting to sit properly on the chair.

'Nothing. Just...she was different? This girl?'

'Luce,' Ben said, automatically. 'And I don't know what you mean.'

'You said she was an old friend,' Seb clarified, and a sense of relief came over Ben.

'Yeah. We knew each other in university. So what?'

'Nothing,' Seb said again.

Ben didn't believe him. Time to change the subject. 'So—come on. I've driven through snowstorms and London traffic to get here. What did you want to meet with me about?'

Seb blinked, tapping a pen against his desk as if trying to remember. Finally he said, 'I've got a new job for you. If you're interested.'

'A "your mission, should you choose to accept it" type thing?' He hoped so. Preferably something far away, completely absorbing and with no reminders of Luce. That sounded pretty much perfect.

'Sort of.' Seb sighed. 'Look. I'm trying to find the right way to say this.'

'Sounds ominous.'

'I don't want you thinking you're not good at your job.'

'I am excellent at my job,' Ben said. 'And since when do you worry about my ego?'

'Since when do you take women to your cottage?' Seb countered.

'Just say it. Whatever it is.'

'Okay. So... Although you are passably good at your job—'

'Excellent at, I think I said.'

'You don't love it.'

Ben looked at his brother in surprise. 'It's a job, Seb. I don't have to love it. I just have to do it.'

'Maybe not. But I think you could love it.'

Things started to fall into place for Ben. 'I know what this is. You're worried that I'm still angry Dad left control of the business to you. I told you—I don't want it. Too much responsibility for me. I like the travel. I like the money. I like making things happen. I don't want to be stuck behind that desk for the rest of my life.'

'Like you think I will be?' Seb looked at him. 'You think I'm going to turn into Dad.'

'Not if you choose not to.' Ben shrugged. 'Besides, it's different. You haven't got a wife and kids like Dad did.'

'Maybe I'd like to have those things, though. One day.'

'Really?' Ben shook his head. 'Nah—can't see it. You'll sit there and manage the business, I'll go out and about and make things happen, and neither of us will drag any kids from boarding school to hotel for their entire childhood. It's all good.'

'And that would be enough for you?'

'Yeah. Of course it would. What are you thinking? That I need a private jet to make my life complete?'

'Honestly? I think you need a home. I think you need someone to come home to. I know everything with Mum screwed up that ideal for you, and maybe it was easier for me, being away at boarding school already. But it wasn't your problem to fix. You can't fix problems, only situations. And, Ben, it's time to move on. Time to grow up at last.'

But Seb hadn't seen it. Hadn't seen their mother falling apart day by day. He'd already been away, engrossed in school and friends and sport. He'd already moved on before Mum had.

Ben had been the only one there to try to make things right for her. And he hadn't been able to.

'I think you're crazy.' Pushing against the arms of the chair, Ben stood up. 'And if that's all you wanted to talk to me about—'

'I haven't finished.' When Ben remained standing, Seb sighed. 'Just sit down, Ben. I promise to stay on topic. Business only. Your shambles of a private life is your own.'

'Yeah, like yours is any better,' Ben grumbled. But he sat.

'I'm working on it,' Seb said with a lopsided smile.

'Really? Am I missing something here? Did something happen while I was away?'

'Business only, right?' Seb grabbed a folder from the corner of his desk and handed it across to Ben.

Opening the file, Ben felt his heart lurch against his ribcage at the sight of the reception desk at the Royal Court Hotel, Chester. *So much for a distraction from Luce.* Slamming the folder shut, he said, 'Been there. Done that. What's next?'

'I want you to go back.'

'Why? It's fine. It's running well. I've made my recommendations for streamlining some processes, making things more effective. Other than that...' He shrugged.

'I want to try something new.'

Against his better judgement, curiosity welled up in Ben. Something new. Something different. That was something they'd never been able to do while their father was alive. He'd had an unalterable system. Buy the hotel, make it look and run like all the others in the chain, move on to the next project. Every time.

'New how, exactly?'

Seb gave him a slow smile. 'Knew that would catch your attention. Trust me, you're going to like this plan.'

Ben wasn't so sure about that. But he was willing to give his brother the benefit of the doubt. 'Okay. I'm listening.'

Luce barely had time to toss her suitcase in her room before her phone rang. Glancing at the display, she saw it was her mother and let it go to voicemail. *Sorry, Mum, but if you want dinner tonight you'll have to wait for me to call you back.*

Okay, it was almost five in the afternoon. Two hours until her guests arrived. Long enough to cook something fantastic if she had any food in the house—which, having missed her supermarket delivery, she didn't. Long enough to clean and tidy the house if she didn't have to do anything else—which she did. And long enough to make herself look presentable if she could bring herself to care what she looked like—which she couldn't.

Collapsing into her favourite armchair, Luce pulled out her organiser and started her list. The most important thing about the evening was that it go well for Tom. After his break-up with Hattie, and the misery and depression that had followed, he'd not introduced them to a new girlfriend in two years. This was big. This was a turning point. Luce needed to make it as successful as she could. And pray that the turkey she'd yanked out of the freezer the moment she walked in defrosted in time for tomorrow.

Obviously at this stage a gourmet feast was out of the question. Instead Luce raided the corner shop for whatever was left at this point in the Christmas panic buying—

mostly mismatched canapés and mince pies. Halfway to the till she remembered to grab vegetables for the next day. She'd just have to hope she had enough of everything else in to make do.

The house itself wasn't in too bad shape—after flinging everything that didn't belong in the lounge, dining room or kitchen into the bedroom, Luce figured it would serve. Candles and cloth napkins on the table, lamps instead of overhead lights, and they were set to go.

Of course by that point it was seven, and she was still wearing the skirt and jumper she'd travelled home from Brecon in. A shower was out of the question, she supposed, but she'd hoped to at least change and put some make-up on. The ringing doorbell suggested she was out of luck.

'Are you running late?' Dolly asked, looking her up and down as she answered the door.

'However did you guess?' Luce ushered her sister in. 'I just got back a couple of hours ago. You're lucky I'm here at all.'

'Tom's lucky, you mean. I had plans for tonight, you know. This new girl of his had better be worth the effort. Does this mean you didn't have time to make the choco-late pots?'

Luce glared, and Dolly held up her hands in self-defence. 'Okay, okay. Next time. You go and get changed and I'll get us something to drink. Is there wine in the fridge?'

'As always,' Luce called back as she went to try to ex-cavate something from her wardrobe that didn't need dry cleaning.

In the end the best option she had turned out to be the purple dress she'd worn to dinner with Ben in Chester. Luce tugged it on, trying not to notice the way his scent still clung to the fabric. Shoving her feet into low heels and pulling a cardigan over it made it feel a little less dressy—

more suitable for a family occasion. *And it matches the culinary sophistication level better. Or maybe I should put on jeans...*

By the time she'd run a brush through her hair and thrown on the minimum amount of make-up her mother would let her get away with, the doorbell had rung twice and Luce could hear voices in the lounge, along with clinking glasses. 'Showtime,' she whispered to herself, and tried not to wish she was still at the cottage.

Five hours later, as Dolly watched her load the dishwasher while eating the leftovers she was supposed to be putting in the fridge, Luce had to admit it had been worth coming back for. Even with her mum's pointed comments about the food.

'Did you think she seemed nice?' Dolly asked.

Since the others had already left, Luce didn't bother hiding the surprise in her voice. 'I did.'

Dolly laughed. 'I know. I wasn't sure whether to expect another monster, or what. But, no, she's nice. A little bossy, maybe. It'll be weird not having Tom here for Christmas Day, though.'

'It will. But he seemed happy.' That was by far the most important part. Tom hadn't been remotely happy for a very long time.

'He did.'

Dolly paused, and Luce looked up at her, forehead creasing.

'You don't.'

'I'm fine,' Luce lied.

Dolly boosted herself up onto the kitchen counter. 'What happened this week?'

'I went away. To a conference. And ended up taking a bit of a detour home, what with all the snow.'

'And were you alone?' Dolly pressed, eyebrows raised.

'Not entirely.' The memory of Ben kissing her against the castle wall invaded her mind and she bit her lip and tried to concentrate on her little sister, in the here and now.

'I knew it! Who did you go with? Oh, no—it wasn't Dennis, was it? That would explain why you're so miserable.'

'It was *not* Dennis,' Luce said, with feeling. 'Wait—I thought you liked Dennis?'

Dolly rolled her eyes. 'Mum liked Dennis. And only because she thought he was what you wanted. Boring, staid and uneventful. But if you weren't with Dennis...'

'My train got cancelled and an old university friend offered me a lift home. We got stuck in the snow and holed up at a cottage in the hills for a couple of days.' She shrugged. 'That's all.'

But Dolly wasn't content to leave it at that. The same curiosity that drove Luce to discover the past had made her sister incurably nosy about the present. 'And was this friend male or female?'

'Does it matter?'

'Yes!' Dolly bounced down from the counter, her eyes bright and intense. 'If you're finally getting a life I want to know all about it. Hell, I want to throw a party in celebration.'

'It's not... There's nothing to celebrate.' Because she was probably never going to see Ben again.

Dolly's mouth turned down at the corners, her eyes full of sympathy. 'Do you want to—? Ooh, I bet that's him!' she interrupted herself as Luce's phone rang.

'I doubt it— *Oh.*' Ben's name flashed across the screen. Of course he'd have programmed his number in on one of the many occasions when he'd stolen her phone. No respect for personal boundaries, that man.

Dolly had already swept up her coat and bag and was halfway out through the door. 'I'll be along tomorrow for my Christmas dinner,' she said with a wave.

Luce stared at the phone again. And then she pressed 'answer'.

# CHAPTER THIRTEEN

IT WENT AGAINST all his usual rules about women and re-
lationships, but Ben needed to talk to someone. And for
some reason the only person he wanted to talk to was Luce.

He sprawled across his bed, waiting for her to answer,
wondering if she would just ignore it. It was late, after all.
Gone midnight. She might be asleep. Or maybe her dinner
party was still going on. Maybe Dennis of the annoying
e-mails was there. Maybe—

'Hello?'

Maybe she would answer after all.

'Hey. Merry Christmas. You okay?'

'Happy Christmas to you, too.' There was a rustle of
fabric on the other end of the phone. Was she in bed? 'I'm
okay. Tired.'

'How did dinner go?' That was what you did, wasn't
it? When you wanted someone to stay in your life even if
just as a friend? You asked about stupid things you didn't
care about.

'You can't tell me that you're suddenly interested in my
family gatherings after all the time you've spent malign-
ing them this week.'

Luce's voice was amused, but Ben could hear a sharper
edge under it. He'd hurt her, even though he'd tried so
hard not to.

'No, not really.' Ben sighed. 'I just don't understand why it was so much more important to you than…everything else.'

'Because you never asked,' Luce responded promptly.

She had a point. Unfortunately, he'd found, she usually did. 'Okay, then, I'm asking. What was so important about this dinner?'

'Hang on,' she said.

Ben heard the click of her phone being put down somewhere. There was more rustling, then she picked up the phone again.

'Were you just getting undressed?' Ben asked, the image waking up his exhausted body instantly.

Luce gave a low laugh. 'It's gone midnight and I am more than ready to be out of this dress. Besides, if we're going to have this conversation I want to be comfortable while we're doing it.'

'What conversation?' The word made Ben nervous. He usually tried to avoid being in any situation with a woman that required him to have a serious conversation.

'The one about my family and why you're so offended by my taking care of them. And don't think I didn't notice that we managed to *not* have this conversation at any point where we couldn't just hang up on each other.'

'Well, we were a little preoccupied at certain points.'

'Ben?'

'Yeah?'

'We are not having phone sex.'

*Damn.* 'I know that. So—go on. Tell me about this dinner.'

Luce sighed. 'It wasn't just a dinner. It was for my brother Tom. He's had a rough time of it the last few years. Longer, really. But when his marriage broke down a couple of years ago he totally fell apart. And because he was in such a state my mother was beside herself, too. It was just when Dolly was applying to drama schools and, well...'

'You got stuck trying to hold everyone together?'

'Yeah. Anyway, this was the first time since then that Tom's met someone he's wanted to introduce us to. First time he's seemed interested in anything, let alone anyone, since Hattie left him.'

'And you didn't want to risk it not happening?'

'I just... It was a big deal for my family. And he'll be with her tomorrow. This was our only chance to be all together.'

'I get that.' Ben thought about Luce, alone in that big house, trying to make her family happy so that she could finally relax enough to find some happiness herself. 'I guess I just don't get why they're all *your* responsibility.'

'Who else would look after them?'

It was a throwaway comment, Ben knew. Self-deprecating, accepting the inevitable. But could he hear a real question under it? Was she ready to cast off some responsibility?

'Maybe it's time they learned to look after themselves.'

'Maybe.' She didn't sound entirely convinced, but it was a start. 'Did you make your meeting with your brother in the end?'

'I did.' It was the reason he'd called, actually. 'He has some new ideas for the business. A new role he wants me to take on.'

'Sounds interesting.'

'It is.'

'You don't sound sure.'

'It's a lot to take on.'

'A big responsibility.' To her credit, she didn't mock him for that. 'Tell me about it.'

How to explain? 'Well, you have to understand when my dad ran the business it was all about turnover. He bought up a hotel, made it a functional and decent place for businessmen, then moved on to the next one. Over time they became higher and higher end, with more amenities and luxurious surroundings, but the basis was the same. It was somewhere to work.'

'And that's where you grew up?' Luce said, surprising him with the sympathy in her voice. 'That must have been—'

'It was fine,' Ben interrupted. 'I got to travel the country before I was ten and the world before I was twenty. Not many kids had that chance.'

'No, but most kids had a home instead of a hotel.'

She sounded as if she wanted to ask more questions, and Ben really wasn't in the mood to be psychoanalysed, so he moved on quickly.

'Anyway, Seb wants to change the model. He wants us to look at adding more boutique hotels to our chain. Maybe even some family-friendly ones.'

'That sounds great. He wants *you* to run this?'

She sounded surprised, but Ben was too tired to be offended. 'Starting with the Royal Court in Chester.' Ben closed his eyes, remembering Seb saying, *Just because you're good at doing what Dad did, it doesn't mean it's what you have to do. It doesn't always have to be about the quick fix and moving on. I think you'll enjoy the challenge of long-term development more.'*

Was he right? Ben supposed he'd find out soon enough.

'So you're heading back to Chester?' Luce asked.

'Not yet. Got to visit some of our hotels on the continent first. But I should be able to get there in a few weeks.'

'So you'll be away a while?'

'About a month.' Normally the idea of getting away, of waking up in a different city every few days, would be appealing. Especially after an interlude with a woman who was getting too close for comfort. But today…it seemed too long.

There was a lengthy pause, and Ben cast around for something else to say to keep her on the phone. It had been so much easier when they were in the cottage, shut away from the rest of the world. Where he'd had her all to himself without having to share her.

'Should I…?' He took a deep breath and started again. 'Can I call you when I get back?'

Luce's voice was soft as she replied, 'Yes, please.'

Luce was surprised, in a way, at how easily she slipped back into her old life. Her pre-Ben life. There was no reason to be, she supposed. After all, she'd lived without Ben in her life for a lot longer than when he'd been there. But still, those few days at the cottage had been transformative, somehow. She wasn't the same person she'd been before she went. Even if it wasn't obvious in her everyday life.

'What are these files?' Dolly asked, poking at a stack of folders on the dining room table a few weeks later, when she came over to indulge in Luce's tea—and her biscuit tin.

Luce glanced over. 'Just some stuff Dennis wants me to sort through for him.'

Dolly raised her eyebrows. 'And this is more important than your own work because…?'

'It isn't.' Luce swept the files into a box on the nearby dining chair. 'That's why I haven't done them yet.' Besides, Dennis was still sulking about her missing the lecture in Chester. Given the way she'd snapped at him when he whined, he probably wouldn't be asking her to do anything else for him any time soon.

'Good.' Dolly settled herself onto one of the other chairs, tipping it back to rest against the wall behind her. 'You've changed, you know. In a good way,' she added hurriedly. 'But you definitely seem different since you went away last month.'

Luce stopped tidying. 'Do I?'

'Yeah.' Dolly slanted her head to the side and looked her up and down for long enough to make Luce blush. 'Maybe more self-assured, I guess. Which is good.'

'More self-aware, I think.' Luce bit her lip as she considered her sister.

She needed to tell someone her news, and Ben was still away. She'd thought about calling a few times, always late at night when she was tucked up in bed, but she couldn't tell him this over the phone. It wasn't fair. But Dolly... She seemed more of an ally than she ever had before lately. She'd always been the baby, the one who needed the most looking after, but recently she'd been more of a friend than an obligation. Someone who cared about Luce rather than just needing things from her. She could tell Dolly.

'What's going on?' Dolly let her chair tip onto four legs again, leaning forward to rest her wrists on her knees. 'Come on—tell me. It's obviously something big. You're actually blushing.'

Luce's face grew immediately hotter in response. 'Okay. But you can't tell Mum. Or Tom. Or anybody just yet.'

Dolly's eyes widened. 'Now I'm *really* intrigued.'

Gripping the edge of the table, Luce summoned her courage and said it out loud for the first time. 'I'm pregnant.'

For a long moment Dolly just stared at her in silence. Then she clapped her hand over her mouth, not quite muffling the squeak that came out.

Luce sank into a chair. 'I know. I know. It's absurd.'

'It's wonderful!' Jumping up, Dolly wrapped her arms around her, and Luce relaxed into the hug. 'I'm going to be an aunt!'

'You are,' Luce said firmly. She'd considered the other options—of course she had. But this was her baby—hers and Ben's—and it might be her only chance. She was financially capable of looking after it, she had her family around her...

'God, how the hell are you going to baby-proof this place?' Dolly asked, looking around.

...and she lived in a death trap.

'That's on my list of things to figure out,' Luce said. 'To be honest, given the length of the list, it might take me a while to get around to it.'

Dolly perched on the table beside her, looking down through her long dark hair. 'Okay, I'm not asking the obvious question, because I figure you'll tell me when it's right. But just promise me it's not Dennis's.'

Luce laughed. 'Trust me. The father is about as far from Dennis as you can imagine.'

'In that case, I really want to meet him,' Dolly said. 'I take it it's the old university friend, then? The one you got snowed in with?'

Luce nodded. 'That's him.'

'Funny...I didn't even know you were still in touch with any of your friends from then.'

'You mean, you didn't know I had any in the first place.' She hadn't, really. Mandy had been her housemate, but had only been friendly when it suited her.

'That, too.'

'We weren't...close then.' Understatement of the year.

Dolly nudged her with her shoulder. 'You obviously are now. Have you told him?'

God, how had things changed so that Dolly was the one asking sensible questions? Luce had imagined this conversation the other way round all through Dolly's teenage years. 'Not yet. He's away on business. I don't want to tell him over the phone.'

'Fair enough. How do you think he'll react?'

Luce thought of Ben recounting his life rules over dinner in Chester, his explanation of the one-night rule, and said, 'Badly.'

Really, who wouldn't? Yes, he'd asked if he could call her when he got back from his business trip, but that wasn't the same as having a lifetime tie to another person and the responsibility of a baby thrust upon him. Of course he was going to react badly. It was what he did next, once he'd calmed down, that mattered. How would he try to fix her life this time? Because if his answer was to throw money at the problem, rather than time or love, she was done with Ben Hampton.

'Then he's an idiot. Clearly having you in his life would be the best thing to ever happen to him.'

Luce looked up, astonished. 'Thank you.'

'And, anyway, it doesn't matter what he says. Auntie Dolly will be here to make things brilliant every step of the way.'

To her surprise, Luce found that made her feel a whole lot better.

Ben stared up at the building of the Royal Court Hotel, the February wind whipping down the cobbled streets and through his coat. How the hell was he going to look at this place objectively, think about changing anything, without thinking about Luce? Hell, she was all he'd thought of for over a month. In every Hampton & Sons hotel he'd visited there'd been something to remind him of her. A bedspread or a cushion in the same soft fabric she loved. A gin and tonic at the bar. Shining dark hair glimpsed across a room. She was haunting him, and he couldn't even figure out why. Was it because he'd left her as broken as he'd found her? Maybe more so? Or was it as simple as a bruised ego? He'd offered to break his rules for her and she'd turned him down.

He'd considered finding someone else—someone to prove the validity of his one-night rule—but none of the women he'd met seemed to appeal. Nothing did. Not the New Year's Eve party he'd found himself at in New York, nor the cutting-edge restaurant in Sydney. And as the jobs dragged on and delays crept in all he wanted was to be back in his cottage. With Luce.

He'd even thought about calling, asking her to join him, but he couldn't bear to hear her say that she couldn't leave her family, her job, whatever else it was that mattered more than he did.

The woman might think she wanted to settle down, find true love, but until she cut those ties—or at least slackened them a little—no man stood a chance.

Besides, it wasn't as if *he* was looking to settle down anyway. His job—his life—still involved travelling the world, getting out there, and what woman would put up with that long-term?

*She could come with me. Write on the road...* Except she wouldn't. And so he wouldn't ask. Even if the thought of waking up next to Luce Myles every morning was incredibly tempting.

Shivering, Ben pushed open the door at last, and memories made him grit his teeth at the sight of the lobby. The desk where he'd first seen her. The bar where he'd stolen her diary. And, upstairs, the suite where she'd taken that long, long bath. God, knowing what he knew now, he wished he'd just walked in on her then. All that time wasted...hours and hours when he could have had her in his arms and hadn't.

And even more of them ahead.

'Mr Hampton!'

The blonde behind the reception desk beamed at him and Ben tried desperately to remember her name.

'It's so wonderful to have you back so soon.'

Which meant that the entire hotel staff were panicking about why he needed a repeat visit, and wondering if it was a sign that their jobs were in danger. *Great.* 'It's lovely to be back…'

'Daisy.'

'Daisy. Right.' Ben rubbed a hand over his aching forehead. 'Sorry—long flight.'

A look of carefully schooled concern settled onto her face. 'Why don't we get you checked in, then, sir? I've put aside the King James Suite for you again, if that's okay?'

'Wonderful,' Ben said, taking the key. Not a chance in hell of getting any sleep there without Luce beside him. *Great.*

Even the walk to the lift was full of memories. Ben distracted himself by watching the other guests instead, trying to observe them in a professional manner, figure out their wants and needs and how the hotel could meet them.

The businessmen by the bar were easy; Ben's father had known exactly what they needed. A comfortable room, with a desk or table to work at, all-night concierge and room service, meeting rooms and wireless internet access, a business centre with photocopiers and fax machines, and admin assistants they could hire by the hour. A well-stocked bar and well-served restaurant. All done. The Royal Court had them covered. Of course so did every other business hotel in every city.

But what about the couple canoodling by the pot plant? What did they want?

Well, if they were anything like him and Luce...privacy, a sturdy bed, champagne in the mini-bar, a big, deep bath. Maybe a romantic restaurant for dinner, breakfast from room service. Nothing unusual. And, honestly, the couple by the plant were so wrapped up in each other that it didn't look as if it mattered where they were, as long as they had each other.

Which just left him wondering why he and Luce had never managed that. Which was depressing. Time to move on.

But the family waiting by the lift, with two huge suitcases and a small boy with an oversized rucksack... They didn't look happy.

The father was in a suit, tie knotted tightly, jacket still on, briefcase in hand. This wasn't a man who'd left work and gone straight on holiday with his family. This was a man who was still working. And, from the frown creasing his wife's forehead, she wasn't too happy about it. The boy just looked miserable.

Ben knew that look. That was the *another day, another hotel* look. The *will I get to see my dad between meetings?* look. The *did I bring enough books to read?* look. That boy knew his family weekend was going to be spent watching his parents arguing, then his mother putting on a brave face while his father disappeared to yet more meetings.

Ben had been that boy. And Ben knew what would happen when the mother couldn't take any more.

He couldn't change another family's future—couldn't explain to every father dragging his wife and kids to business hotel after business hotel instead of actually taking a holiday what could happen and how it felt. But maybe he could make it a little more fun for the families waiting for their husbands, wives, mothers or fathers to finish their meetings.

Pulling his mobile from his pocket, he called his brother. 'Seb? That new style of hotel you wanted? I've got an idea.'

## CHAPTER FOURTEEN

IT HAD BEEN eight weeks. He'd said he'd be away for a month, and now it was nearly two. Luce dropped her bag by the front door and collapsed onto the sofa, preparing herself for another evening of not hearing from Ben.

Damn him.

She should have known better than to believe him when he said he'd call. Hadn't he made it perfectly clear what they were? One night only. He wasn't going to call again.

But eventually she'd have to call him. He deserved to know.

Her head ached, her body was exhausted, and constant low-level nausea left her weak and miserable—and, damn it, she wanted to tell him! Wanted the secret off her shoulders. Wanted to share it with someone else.

Dolly knew, of course, and had been more wonderful than Luce had imagined possible. Her little sister had grown up unexpectedly, and Luce loved seeing this new, responsible side to her. Having her onside made things bearable. But soon she would have to tell other people— her boss, her mother, Tom. God, she'd even have to tell Dennis eventually. But Ben had to know first.

She'd have to call him. If he wasn't back soon she'd have to tell him over the phone. Except then she wouldn't be able to see his face, his reaction, the truth about how he felt.

She'd imagined it a dozen different ways. Sometimes, if she was feeling excessively romantic, he fell down on one knee and proposed instantly. Most of the time he looked shocked, stunned and slightly horrified. That was okay. She expected that. But sometimes, after that, her imagination had him take her in his arms and tell her they'd figure it out together. And sometimes it had him walk out without looking back.

She'd cope, whatever his reaction—she knew that. She just needed to know what it was. If he wanted to be involved in his child's life or not. Then she could start making plans. Until then…this horrible limbo persisted.

Time to move the action back into her own hands. *Take responsibility. Take control.* 'If he doesn't call tonight I'll phone him.'

'You've been saying that for weeks,' Dolly said from the door.

Sad, but true. 'Yeah, but now I'm desperate. I'll do it.'

Dolly sighed, shut the front door behind her and came to sit on the sofa, lifting Luce's feet to rest them on her lap.

'Has it occurred to you that you might be better off without him? I mean, he's basically disappeared off the face of the earth for two months now, Luce.'

'I know. And it has.' Luce sighed. 'Chances are he'll run like the wind when I tell him anyway. But he needs to know. And *I* need to know.'

'This is all because you can't write your "To Do" list before you tell him, isn't it?'

Luce chuckled. 'Partly.'

Dolly tilted her head to look at her. 'Are you in love with him?'

Rolling her eyes, Luce gave her sister a shove to the shoulder. 'You've asked the same question every day for two months now. What on earth makes you think my answer might have changed? No, I'm not in love with him. But he's the father of my child, and the responsible thing is to let him know that and have a conversation about whether he wants to be involved. That's all.'

Dolly's smile was sad. 'I think you're getting less convincing every time you say that. Come on—I'll make us some tea.'

The worst thing was Dolly was right. As ridiculous as Luce knew it was to have fallen in love with someone based on three days in a cottage in the middle of nowhere, she was starting to be very afraid that was what had happened.

She missed him. More than she'd thought she possibly could. When he'd called that first night she'd hoped that maybe they'd speak again while he was away. Then, when he hadn't called, she'd been grateful for a while—after she took the pregnancy test and realised she had to tell him in person. She hadn't been sure she could keep it from him if they spoke.

But now? Now she just ached to see him. She fell asleep wishing she had his arms around her and woke up missing his morning kisses and the way, the one morning they'd woken up together, the first thing he'd done was pull her closer, kissing her neck. She missed the way he told her she had to stop working sometimes, to relax and have fun.

And she really wished he was around to help her figure out what to do about Tom.

Dolly brought the tea tray back to the coffee table: thick slices of ginger cake on a plate next to the teapot, milk jug and cups. 'I picked this up from the deli down the road. They said the ginger should be good for nausea.'

'Smells wonderful.' Luce picked up her plate and took a slice. Still warm.

Once she'd poured the tea Dolly settled into the armchair on the other side of the armchair. 'Okay. Now that you're fed and watered we need to talk.'

'Look, Doll, I'm going to tell him. But—'

Dolly put up a hand to stop her. 'Not about that, for once. We need to talk about Tom.'

Luce sank back against the cushions and ate some more cake. 'I know we do. I just—'

'Don't want to. I understand.' Dolly took a deep breath. 'I think you need to tell him about the pregnancy.'

'How on earth would *that* help?'

'He's talking to Mum about how he and Vanessa should have the house. Since she's got kids already and they need the space.'

Luce blinked. 'But it's *my* house. Grandad left it to me. And besides, they've been together—what?—three months? And they're already talking about shacking up in *my* home with *her* kids?' Luce could hear her voice getting higher and squeakier as she talked, but she couldn't seem to stop herself.

'Okay, you need to calm down. Think of the baby.'

Luce rolled her eyes, but settled back obediently against the cushions. 'As if I think about anything else.' Except the baby's father.

'Look, I don't know if he's just testing the waters, or what. But Mum's so happy to see him settled with someone that I think she'll go for anything that keeps him that way.'

'But it's my house,' Luce repeated, calmer this time.

'I know. But you've always given in to them before. To me, too.'

'You make it sound like I'm a doormat.'

'It's not that. It's just that you're always working so damn hard to make sure we're all happy and okay.'

'And that's a bad thing?'

'Not in itself, no. But Mum and Tom...they expect it now. They can't imagine it any other way.'

Everything Ben had ever said about giving in to her family, about giving up her life for them, came back in a rush. He was right. He'd been right all along. This was her life, and she needed to live it for herself. And she'd have someone else even more important to live it for when the baby came. She'd have her own little family to be responsible for. She couldn't let her mother and brother run her life any more.

'You honestly think they expect me to give up the house?'

Dolly shrugged. 'Mum and Tom both treat this place like it's theirs anyway, when it's convenient.'

'Not when the roof almost caved in or the stairs needed replacing.' Funny how they'd been nowhere to be seen when she'd needed money or time to help fix the place up.

'Exactly.'

'Exactly...what?'

'They have no idea what they'd be taking on. But Tom's so used to you doing whatever he needs I don't think it's crossed his mind that you won't just happily move out into some little flat somewhere while he moves his instant family in here.'

'That's crazy!'

'Luce...' Dolly put her cup and saucer back on the tray, and leant forwards. 'You've never said no to him before. No one has—except Hattie, and look what happened then.'

'So you're saying I should give him my house to avoid his mental breakdown?'

'Hell, no!' Dolly shook her head violently, her long dark hair flying across her face. 'I'm saying it's time you *did* say no. Unless you want to get the hell out of this crumbling museum before the baby comes. In which case, make him buy it from you.'

Luce looked around her at the antique furniture, the threadbare rugs and the splintering floorboards. Yes, the place was falling apart. But it was her home—would be her baby's home. It was all she had left of her grandfather. He'd left it to *her*, not to Tom or Dolly or their mother, and he'd done that for a reason.

No way in hell she was parting with it.

'No. It's my home. I'm staying.'

'Fine. Then we need to make that clear to Tom. And then we need to go and buy some yellow paint for the nursery.'

Dolly clapped her hands together with excitement. Luce wasn't sure whether it was the painting or the standing up to Tom that was filling her with glee. It didn't matter.

'There's something else I need to do first,' she said. 'I need to tell Ben.'


Ben was wrestling with the hotel key card when his phone rang. As the door fell open he dropped his suitcase and put the phone to his ear.

'How did it go?' Seb asked.

Ben kicked the door shut behind him. 'It went well, I think.' Meetings with investors were usually Seb's domain, but he'd insisted Ben take this one. It was his baby, after all.

'Good. Full debrief when I get there tomorrow? I got Sandra to book us a meeting room.'

'Sure. Just need to get some sleep first.'

Seb laughed. 'Welcome to the world of real work, brother.'

The cell was cut off as Seb hung up, and Ben tossed the phone onto the coffee table. There was truth in Seb's words. This was *real* work—trying to expand and transform a hotel chain that had been stuck in one mindset for too long. It was work Ben would never have been allowed to do while their father was alive—work he hadn't even known he wanted to do until Seb had suggested it to him.

But now? He was good at this. Better than he'd used to be. Because he cared about making these hotels right for their guests. Not just the businessmen or the couples. He wanted a chain of boutique hotels that felt like a home away from home for the families that stayed in them. That made the kids feel safe and happy—not scared of another sterile white room with a too-big bed. Not a free-for-all family hotel with everything in red plastic either, though. This was a hotel for grown-ups, too. It just didn't exclude or alienate children.

He had a plan, and he had convinced the backers, but he had a hell of a lot of work ahead of him.

But first he needed to sleep.

The phone rang again before he could make it to the bedroom. He intended to ignore it until he saw the name flashing across the screen.

*Luce.*

Snatching the phone up, he said, 'Hey, I was going to ring you. I just got back into the country and I'm in Cardiff for a few days.' He didn't mention that he'd scheduled this particular leg of the trip in the hope of getting to see her.

'That's lucky,' she said, her voice warm and familiar. 'I really need to talk to you.'

'Okay. Want to do it over the phone? Or meet me for lunch tomorrow?'

'Um...neither. Look, could I come over? Where are you staying?'

Ben felt ready to drop. His eyes itched with grit and his very bones ached with tiredness. But the thought of Luce in his arms again... 'Of course. I'd love to see you.'

There was a sigh of relief at the other end and Ben felt the first pang of concern at the sound. What did she want to talk about, anyway? He *had* hoped whatever it was was an excuse—just a reason to see him. He'd have to wait and see, he thought as he rattled off the hotel's details for Luce. She'd be here soon enough, and he really needed to shower first.

He barely made it. The knock on the door came as he towelled off his hair. Pulling a tee shirt over his head, he padded barefoot to the door in the comfiest jeans he'd packed and hoped Luce wouldn't be too disappointed if he wasn't up to hours of bedtime fun tonight.

When he opened the door he stopped worrying about that and started worrying about her instead. Her hair was scraped back from her face and he could clearly see the redness around her eyes, the puffiness of her skin.

'Are you okay? You look dreadful.' He ushered her in, keeping an arm around her shoulders as he guided her to the sofa.

Luce gave a watery chuckle. 'Just what every girl likes to hear.'

'Sorry. But…what's happened?'

'God—everything.' She sighed. 'Um…my brother Tom.'

'The one you rushed back to cook a dinner for?' Ben tried to keep the censure from his voice. He wasn't sure he was entirely successful, though.

'Yeah, that was… I shouldn't have. I know that now.'

Ben blinked at the unexpected victory. Except if she'd changed her mind *that* thoroughly… 'What did he do?'

'He wants my house.'

'What?'

Luce rubbed at her eyes. 'He and his new partner want to move in together, with her two kids, and Tom thinks it's only fair that *they* get the family house, since there's more of them.'

'That's crazy. It's your home.'

'That's what I'm going to tell him. And...'

She trailed off, and Ben felt fear clutch at his insides. What else had her brother done? 'Go on. Tell me.'

Luce looked up at him, holding his gaze with her own. Her eyes still looked tired and watery, but they were clear as she said, 'I need to tell him I'm pregnant. But I couldn't do that until I'd told you. That's why I wanted to see you tonight.'

'You need to tell him... Wait—what?' The world seemed to have gone fuzzy. Luce's voice was buzzing in his ear, making it impossible to make out the words. 'But... What?'

'I'm pregnant.' The words cut through the haze of confusion, clear as a bell, but still Ben couldn't make sense of them.

'Pregnant?' he repeated numbly.

'Yeah. I know we used protection, but that first time...'

'I was too desperate for you.' Stumbling to his feet, Ben moved to lean against the back of the sofa, hands braced against the edge, staring down at the cream leather. 'God, this is just...'

'I know it's not what either of us planned,' Luce said from behind him.

She sounded brave, calm—but then, she'd had more time to figure all this out, hadn't she? How long had she known? Long enough to make a twenty-five-point plan for dealing with it, he was sure. Whereas here he was, half-asleep and dead on his feet, trying to get his mind around the idea that in seven months he would be a *father*.

God, how could he be? When he'd just promised Seb he'd take on the whole new business? He couldn't drag Luce and a baby from hotel to hotel with him, like his father had. He'd lose them in a heartbeat. And Luce would never trail around after him while he worked anyway. She had her own career, and her own family tying her to Cardiff. He wasn't foolish enough to think she'd give those up for a man she barely knew and had spent just a few days with, even if she was mad at her brother right now.

So what did that leave?

Luce touched him on the shoulder and he flinched in surprise, spinning round to see her watching him with wide eyes. 'Look, I know this is a surprise—'

'Surprise?' Ben shook his head. 'It's a shock. A disaster.'

Her face hardened at that, and he wanted to take it back, but it was the truth, after all. What was he going to *do*?

'Okay. Fine. I just wanted you to know so you could decide what involvement you want in your child's life. Obviously the answer to that is clear. So I'll just—'

'Wait. No. I just… I need a little time here, Luce.'

She nodded. 'That's understandable. Why don't I meet you for lunch, later in the week, and we can talk? Come up with a plan?'

'No! I don't want you to go. And I don't want to come up with a plan! This is our whole lives being turned upside down. A "To Do" list isn't going to fix that.'

'It's a start.'

'It's an end. It's giving up on any other options.'

Her face turned stony. 'Options?'

Ben stared at her, his eyes widening when he realised what she thought he meant. 'Not that. No, never that. I just… I don't know how we could make this work right now. The business… There's a lot going on right now, and Seb needs me to do it…'

Luce took a step back, her mouth twisted in a cruel smile. 'So now your work matters to you? Right.'

'There's a new project,' Ben started, but it sounded weak even to his own ears.

How could he explain to her again, in a way she'd understand, that he couldn't be the man his father had been? He couldn't lose her and his child that way, have them hating him for never being there. But he still had too much to do. He couldn't give up his dreams for a life in an office, nine to five, never going anywhere or seeing anything. Where would they even live? A never-ending series of hotel rooms would be terrible for a child, despite the new project, and by all accounts her house was falling apart. They didn't even have a home—how could they be a family?

'I just need some time, Luce.'

She shook her head. 'No. You've made your priorities very clear, thanks. I can do this on my own. I have my family to help me.'

'Would that be the same family that's trying to take your home away from you? And how the hell are you going to look after a baby in that place anyway?'

'What? You think we'd be better off here?'

She glanced around her and Ben knew she was taking in the sharp corners and sterile white and metal furnishings. Nothing like the cottage at all.

'I think you'd be better off with me.'

'Living out of hotel rooms? Never settling down? Isn't that what you said you'd *never* do to a child?' The words stung as she bit them out. 'Or will it be you, gone for months on end, sleeping with every woman who smiles at you in a hotel bar? No, thanks. A family takes more than a one-night rule, Ben.'

He swallowed back an angry denial, not least because he knew everything she said was true. His father hadn't been able to do it, and Seb wasn't even trying, for all his talk. Ben wasn't content to be one of those once-a-month visiting dads. So maybe Luce was right. Maybe there was no place for him at all.

'I can help. Financially.'

She threw him a scathing look. 'I don't want it,' she said. Ben heard, *I don't want you.*

'Money isn't going to give you a quick fix this time.'

Why was he even surprised? he wondered as Luce walked out, slamming the door behind her. He'd never expected his father to love him more than his work, or his mother to love him more than her freedom. He certainly couldn't expect Luce to love him more than her child.

*Their* child.

'Hell,' he whispered, and went to pour himself a very large whisky from the mini-bar.

# CHAPTER FIFTEEN

LUCE REFUSED TO CRY.

She stayed resolutely dry-eyed while flagging down a taxi. She remained calm as they drove through the dark Cardiff streets and as she paid the driver. She didn't even give in while she fumbled with the keys to get into her house.

But at the sight of Dolly, asleep on her sofa with a blanket over her knees, having obviously failed in waiting up for her to get home, Luce fell apart and sobbed.

Dolly awoke with a start, jerking upright and tossing back the blanket even as she stumbled to her feet. 'What happened?' she asked, her voice bleary.

Luce shook her head and pulled Dolly down to sit on the sofa with her. 'I can't... Just...don't ask, please.'

'Idiot,' Dolly whispered. 'Tell me he wasn't more of an idiot than Tom?'

'It's a toss-up.'

'Useless. All of them. We should run away to some women's commune and raise her there.'

'It might be a boy.'

'Doesn't matter. We'll dress him in skirts.' Dolly shook her head. 'Except then Tom would just steal the house while we were gone, and that's no good. So we'll stay here.'

'We?' Luce blinked up at her sister

Dolly took a deep breath. 'I thought I could move in and help you. If you want me. And not at all in a house-stealing sibling way. Because you already have one of those. I know I haven't always been much help in the past, but I think it might be time for me to grow up and take care of myself.'

Luce tilted her head to look at her sister. 'You *have* grown up. I don't know what changed.'

Dolly shook her head. 'Doesn't matter. The only thing that does is that I want to be here to help you with the baby. To look after you for a change.'

'That would be wonderful.' Relief started to seep into her chest. She didn't have to do this alone. Even if Ben wasn't there she still had Dolly.

'And besides, I thought the rent money might help you with doing this place up a bit. Making it safe for the baby.'

Luce stared at her. 'You don't have to pay rent. You're still my baby sister.'

'And I'm a grown-up now, remember? I can pay my own way.' Dolly smiled a lopsided smile. 'Maybe we can help look after each other. Because it seems to me that there's going to be someone soon who needs your love and care a lot more than me or Tom or Mum.'

'Especially if I'm the only parent it's got.' Luce slumped back against the arm of the sofa.

'Idiot,' Dolly muttered again. 'But it doesn't matter. You'll be the best mum any child could hope for. And I'll be the coolest auntie.'

'Of course.'

There was a pause, then Dolly asked, 'What did he say?'

'He's got a lot of work on at the moment. He offered me money.' That was a reasonable summary, Luce felt.

'How dare he!' Dolly's voice grew ever more vehement. 'The thing is, he's not a bad man. He...he looked shell-shocked at the whole thing. Trapped. Like he couldn't see a way out.'

Dolly shook her head. 'Doesn't matter. He should have manned up and supported you.'

'Yeah, I know.' Luce twisted her hands in the blanket. He should have. Of course he should. And she couldn't quite believe that he hadn't.

'But...?'

Luce looked up at her sister. 'The thing is, I think I might be a little bit in love with him.'

Dolly laughed and pulled her into a hug, her arms warm and comforting around her. 'Oh, Luce. Of course you are. I've known that for weeks.'

'Then how come I only just figured it out?'

'Because you were too busy trying to come up with a sensible plan for all this. Except love isn't sensible, and it can't be planned.'

'Is that why you fall in love so often? Because you're not sensible and can't be planned either?'

'Exactly.'

How had her baby sister grown up so smart? Luce laid her head against Dolly's shoulder and stared out into the darkened room. She knew where every stick of furniture was, exactly where each painting hung on the wall. They'd been there her whole life, after all. 'What do I do now, Doll?'

'You just take each day as it comes. It gets easier, I promise. And I'll help you.'

Luce nodded. Time to try life without a 'To Do' list for a while.

Ben woke feeling jet-lagged and hung-over, and cursed his alarm clock before he'd even opened his eyes. A headache pounded behind his temples, beating a rhythm that sounded like a door slamming over and over again. Still, he had work to do. And since, after last night, work was all he had, he supposed he'd better make the most of it.

Dragging himself out of bed, into the shower and then into a suit took twice as long as normal. He skipped breakfast, his stomach rebelling at the idea. How much had he drunk after Luce had left? The mini-bar looked suspiciously empty.

Seb was waiting for him in the meeting room and raised his eyebrows at the sight of him. 'Jet-lag?' he asked, pouring Ben a coffee.

Ben dropped into an empty chair and pulled the saucer closer. 'Amongst other things.'

'Thought you'd be immune to that by now.'

'Twelve time zones in eight weeks is hard on anyone's body.' Which was true. It just wasn't why Ben felt so awful.

Seb tilted his head, looking sympathetic. 'You need some time off?'

Ben shook his head. 'I need to work.'

'Why?' Seb's brow furrowed. 'What's going on, Ben? You've been different lately. First your trip away with your "university friend" then a sudden desire to revamp our hotels for the family market. Anything you need to tell me?'

'She's pregnant,' Ben said, his voice flat.

Seb's eyebrows shot up. 'Really? Well, that explains a lot. When did you find out?'

'Last night.'

'Oh. So the hotel thing was...?'

'Coincidental. I hadn't seen her since we came back from the cottage. She stopped by last night and told me. I...reacted badly.'

'You were exhausted last night, Ben. I'm sure if you call her, talk to her...'

'No. She's right. It's better that I'm not a part of the baby's life.'

'She said that?' Seb shook his head. 'That can't possibly be true.'

Ben shrugged. 'What could I give a child? I have no idea how to be a father, my job means travelling pretty much all of the time, and I won't force a kid to come along with me like Dad did. This is something I can't fix. She told me as much.'

'You mean you won't try.' Seb's tone was flat. Disappointed.

Ben glared up at him. 'You don't think I would if I could?'

'I think you're scared. I think you've got so used to swooping in and solving a crisis before retiring victorious you've forgotten that some things take more than that. Some things are worth more than that. More than just throwing money at a problem, or hiring and firing people.'

'That's my *job*,' Ben snapped.

'Yeah, and this is your life. Your future. It deserves more than a quick fix. Your child deserves more.' Seb stared until Ben flinched. 'You need to decide right now that you're in this for the long haul.'

The long haul. For ever.

With Luce.

After the last couple of months of being miserable without her, how could he give that up without a fight?

Ben swallowed. 'Okay. Say I'm in. What the hell do I do? She still thinks I'm the same person I was at university, with no sense of responsibility. She thinks I've never grown up.'

'Then maybe it's time to prove her wrong,' Seb suggested.

Ben blinked at his brother. 'What do you mean?'

Seb got to his feet, coming round to lean against the front of the conference table, next to Ben's chair. Ben appreciated the gesture. It made it easier to remember that Seb was his brother, not just his boss, and definitely not their father all over again. Brothers. That was good.

'You're not that kid any more. I remember you at university. You're miles away from that now. You work hard, you value your friends, you want to make a home—'

'Where did you get that one from?' Ben asked with a laugh. 'I live in hotel rooms.'

'Maybe. But I've heard you talk about your cottage. About your plans for the château. What are they, if not homes?'

An image of Luce, leaning against the kitchen counter in the cottage while he cooked, flashed into his mind. Then one of her curled up on the sofa with a book and a blanket. Working at the desk. Sprawled across his bed, smiling at him, waiting for him to join her.

The buildings weren't home. Whatever he did to them, however he filled them, they couldn't be—not on their own.

They needed Luce there. *Luce* was home. Luce and their child.

'Oh, God,' he said, collapsing back in his chair. 'I'm in love with her.'

'Well, I thought that was obvious,' Seb said. 'Now, what do you want to do about it?'

'What *can* I do? She thinks I'm an idiot, and I still can't imagine how I could have a family right now.'

Seb picked up the phone. 'Business Services? Could you get us some more coffee in here, please? And we're going to need the room a little longer than anticipated. We need to have an important planning meeting. Right now.'

'Do you want me to send in some pastries, too?' came the muffled reply. ·

'Definitely,' Seb said, looking at Ben. 'Now, come on. Let's find a way to make this work.'

'I can help with that, you know,' Luce called up the stairs, behind the struggling Dolly and her suitcase. 'I'm pregnant. Not an invalid.'

'You're trying to save me again,' Dolly yelled back.

'No, I'm not. I'm...' But Dolly had already reached the top of the stairs and disappeared into her new bedroom. Since she wasn't allowed to help with any of the fetching and carrying, Luce decided to go and make tea instead. At least that was useful.

As she entered the kitchen her phone rang, as if it had known she was coming. Luce stared at it, sitting on the counter, with Ben's name scrolling across the screen. Just the sight of those three letters made her heart clench. She'd need to talk to him eventually, she knew. Give him another chance for some sort of involvement—with the baby, not her. She was all set without him, thank you. She had her own not-a-plan and she was sticking to it. Just her, Dolly and the baby.

Ben had been right about one thing—even if he was wrong about almost everything else. She needed priorities and she needed to stick to them. And for the foreseeable future her priority was her child, and staying healthy and stress-free so she could look after them.

Neither Ben nor her brother were conducive to that.

The phone stopped ringing and Luce went to put the kettle on. She'd talk to him soon. Just not yet.

'Anyone home?'

Luce's shoulders tensed at the sound of Tom's voice. She hadn't heard his key in the lock, but maybe Dolly had left the door open while she was dragging in her assorted bags and boxes.

'In the kitchen,' she called back, and schooled her face, ready for the showdown.

'Oh, good. I'd murder a cup of tea,' said Tabitha.

Luce bit her lip. She hadn't expected Mum, too. Oh, well, maybe it was best to get it all over with in one go, anyway.

'I'll make a pot,' Luce said. Maybe she could busy herself with the teacups and cake until Dolly came down. Moral support was always appreciated.

'I think that's the last of it,' Dolly said as she entered the kitchen. 'And just in time, too. Hi, Mum. Tom.'

Luce placed the tea tray on the kitchen table. 'Help yourselves,' she said, and settled into the chair at the head of the table.

'Now, Lucinda,' Tabitha said, taking a tiny sliver of cake. 'We wanted to talk to you about Tom's idea. He says you dismissed it rather out of hand, but I don't think you can have listened to all the details. He's put a lot of thought into this, you know.'

'He wants to live in my house with his new girlfriend and her children,' Luce summarised.

'Well, yes. But we thought that you could have Tom's flat in exchange! Wouldn't that be nice? This house is far too big with just you rattling around in it, anyway.'

'Tom's flat is rented,' Luce pointed out. Best to address all the problems with Tabitha's statement in turn, she decided.

'Well, yes, but the rent's very affordable for you on your salary. And, after all, you've been able to live here rent-free for the last few years. Isn't it time Tom had the same opportunity?'

Luce blinked and looked over at Dolly, who appeared

equally baffled by their mother's attempt at reasonable argument.

'She's lived here rent-free because it's *her* house,' Dolly said.

'Only because Grandad left it to her,' Tom put in. 'But it's always been the family house, hasn't it? Luce always says it belongs to all of us, really.'

'Except for the part where it's *her* house. Grandad left you other stuff. And me.'

Dolly's voice grew louder. Her grasp on staying restrained and reasonable wasn't going to last long, Luce suspected.

'Not a house, though,' Tom said, his tone perfectly reasonable.

Luce frowned. 'Is that what this is really about? You're jealous because Grandad left me more valuable property than you?'

Tom straightened his back and stared at her. 'It's not about jealousy. It's about fairness. I need the house more than you, that's all. We're a family. We share.'

The really scary part, Luce thought, was that he truly believed this was a reasonable demand. She'd spent her entire life giving and giving to these people, and now they couldn't imagine that there might be something she wasn't willing to hand over to them.

But Dolly had grown up, grown out of that dependence. She'd changed when Luce had never really believed it was possible.

And that meant Tom could, too.

'Do you know why he left it to me?' Luce asked, mildly.

Tom shook his head.

'He left me a note in the will explaining. He said, *"You're going to spend the rest of your life looking after the lot of them, because God knows they can't do it them-*

*selves. Think of this as your salary."* And I think I've more than earned it over the last few years.'

Tom stared at her, his eyes wide and disbelieving, and Luce squashed down a pang of guilt. She needed to do this. For all their sakes.

'Sounds fair to me,' Dolly said gleefully. 'And that's another reason I have no problem paying you rent.'

'Rent?' Tabitha said, faintly.

'Yep. I'm moving in with Luce. Figure that the rent I pay can help her fix up this place. Trust me, Tom, you wouldn't want the house if you'd seen the damp in the attic.'

Tom finally found his voice. 'But I told Vanessa we could—'

'Well, you shouldn't have,' Luce interjected. 'This is my place, Tom. And while you, and Mum—and Vanessa, if she sticks around—are always welcome here, this is *my* house, *my* home. And I'm afraid all of you are going to have to get better at looking after yourselves. I'm going to have bigger concerns for the next decade or two.'

'Like what?' Tom asked.

'Like my own family. I'm pregnant.'

'You're...? Well... That's lovely, darling, I'm sure.' Tabitha's brows were furrowed, as if she were missing some vital part of the conversation.

Luce wondered if hearing what Grandad had really thought of her had sent Tabitha even further into her own world, reliving past events with new eyes. She was sure her mother would catch up later and demand answers and information. But for now Luce was glad of the respite.

Tom, however, had no such reserve.

'Pregnant! You can't be. Who's the father? Or is this some desperate attempt to find love from a child instead of actually falling in love? Some "must start a family by the age of thirty" plan?'

Anger bubbled in Luce's stomach, acid and biting. She'd known Tom wouldn't take the change in the status quo well, but to hear such words from her own brother—the brother she'd tried so hard to look after and protect—it made her heart ache. And told her it was past time to cut him off. Fighting to keep her voice even she said, 'That's none of your business. Now, get out of my house.'

'I thought we were always welcome here?' Tom said, sneering.

'Not when you talk to her like that, you're not,' Dolly said, grabbing his arm. 'Come on—time to go. Mum, I think you might be better off at home this afternoon, too. We'll see you soon.'

Luce collapsed back in her chair as she heard Dolly bundle their relatives out of the house. Reaching for a piece of ginger cake, she said, 'I can't believe I just kicked them out.'

'I can't believe it took you this long,' Dolly said cheerfully as she sat down and helped herself to her own slice. 'Buck up, sis. You know they'll be back. Tom will calm down and beg for forgiveness, then pretend he never said that stuff. But they need to stand on their own four feet for a while. You did the right thing. And besides, you still have me!'

'Yes, I do,' Luce said. 'And everyone needs an adoring sister to run them a bubble bath from time to time...'

Dolly rolled her eyes. '*Another* bath? Really? Okay. But only because you're pregnant. This stuff stops once the baby's here.'

'That's okay. You can bath the baby then, instead.'

Dolly laughed as she headed off to the bathroom, and Luce thought that maybe, just maybe, things would be okay after all. Not great, perhaps. They couldn't be—not without Ben. But she'd be okay. And that was enough for now.

\* \* \*

*Just one more try.* Ben stared at the phone in his hand for a minute before taking a deep breath and pressing 'call'. Just because she'd ignored his last four phone calls, that didn't mean she'd definitely ignore this one, did it?

Still, as the phone rang and rang, Ben started to have his doubts.

'Hello?'

'Luce?' The voice didn't sound quite right, but international phone lines did that sometimes.

'No, it's Dolly.' The sister. *Great.* 'You must be the "old university friend".'

'Ben Hampton. Is Luce there?'

'She's in the bath. In there all the time now she's pregnant.'

'She was bad enough before.' Ben took a breath, and took a chance. 'Look, I know she's avoiding my calls. I was...'

'An idiot?'

'Last time we spoke. Yes. But I was jet-lagged and exhausted—and stupid, mostly. I've had a chance to let the news sink in, and I'm ready to make it up to her.' Ready to make her the centre of his world if she'd let him.

'Convince me,' Dolly said, her voice firm.

Ben blinked at the phone. 'What?'

'Convince me you're worthy of my sister. Make me want to help you.'

Dolly spoke slowly, as if she thought he was an idiot. Which, actually, she probably did.

'I don't know how.'

'Then try. Or you're on your own.'

Ben stared out across the gardens of the château and thought. He needed this. Needed Dolly's help if he was ever going to get Luce out here and convince her that they could be a real family. But convince her he was worthy of Luce? Impossible.

'I'm not,' he said, finally. 'I'm not worthy of her. Nobody could be.'

'Right answer,' Dolly said. 'Now, tell me your plans and I'll see what I can do. Because, I'm telling you, she's absolutely miserable without you.'

Ben smiled for the first time in a week and told Dolly his plan.

# CHAPTER SIXTEEN

'AT LEAST TELL me where I'm going,' Luce said as Dolly threw more clothes into her suitcase. 'And how long I'll be gone. I need to call work...' Which would be fun. Dennis was still speechless over the pregnancy thing.

'Already done,' Dolly said. 'I told them you'd be back next week. If you decide not to... Well, call them once you're there.'

'Where, exactly?' Luce asked, frustrated. 'And if I'm there longer than a few days that skirt won't fit me any more. Three months and I'm already starting to show.'

'You're glowing,' Dolly said. Then she stopped and looked at her. 'Well, sort of. Right now you just look stressed.'

'I can't imagine why.'

Dolly slammed the lid of the suitcase shut and fastened it, leaning hard on it with her elbow to keep it closed. 'Look, just trust me on this one. It's for the best, and everything's going to work out fine. You need a break. You need looking after. And, most importantly, you need to not be in the house while they're fixing the attic. God only knows what they're going to find up there, and all that dust would be bad for the baby. Even the builder's told you to get out for a few days.'

'I could have just booked into a hotel round the corner for the weekend,' Luce pointed out.

'Except I know you.' Dolly gave her a look. 'You'd be back here every five minutes, wanting to check on things. No. This is my first chance to be the grown-up and in-charge sister, and I'm taking it. I have booked you a long weekend and you are going. End of story. I'll take care of everything here, so you don't need to worry at all.'

Luce opened her mouth to speak, and then closed it again. Telling Dolly she couldn't go, that she'd worry too much, was tantamount to telling her she didn't trust her to look after things. How could she do that when Dolly was trying so hard?

'And, look,' Dolly said, pointing to the carry-on bag next to the suitcase. 'I'm letting you take your research notes and your laptop, aren't I? I know how close you are to finishing the revisions on your book. So it can be a working holiday. Perfect.'

Luce bit her lip at the memory of her last accidental, snowy working holiday. 'Thanks, Doll. I just...'

'You just need to relax. Come on—let's get you to the airport.'

In the end Luce decided it was easier just to cave in to Dolly's boundless enthusiasm and go. A weekend away did sound wonderful, and it was nice to have someone else take care of the planning for a change.

Or so she thought until her plane landed in Nice and there was no one there to meet her.

*This* was why she took care of things herself. As hard as Dolly was trying, organisation and responsibility still didn't come naturally to her. And now Luce was stuck in an airport with no idea where she was supposed to be going.

Fishing her phone out of her bag, she called Dolly. 'I

thought you said there'd be a car here to meet me? With, you know, a driver? To take me to the hotel?'

'He's not *there*?' Dolly's incredulous voice screeched down the line. 'Hang on. I'll call you back.'

Luce took her bags and sat down on a nearby bench to wait. The Arrivals lounge began to empty out a bit, waiting for the next influx of passengers from the following flight, and she glanced around her, trying to see if she'd missed a sign with her name on it or something. Dolly had been so sure it was all arranged...

The doors in front of her opened with a bang, and Luce looked up to see Ben Hampton—paint on his face, jeans, shirt and in his hair—running towards her just as her phone rang.

'Dolly.'

'He's on his way,' Dolly said quickly. 'There was a mix-up—'

'He's already here.'

'Oh.' Dolly paused. 'Are you cross?'

'Possibly. I'll let you know later.'

'Okay.'

Luce hung up. 'You and Dolly came up with a plan. You and Dolly. Together.' The two people least likely to work together or to come up with a coherent, responsible plan.

Wincing, Ben said, 'Yeah. Guess it's no surprise it didn't quite work. I thought you weren't due in for another hour.'

'And you still dressed for the occasion?'

Ben glanced down at his paint-splattered clothes. 'I lost track of time. Come on—let me take your bags.'

'Where are we going?' Luce asked as she followed him out to where his car was parked at a wildly illegal angle on the kerb. 'Another hotel?'

Ben shook his head. 'We're going home.'

* * *

She looked incredible. Three months pregnant, straight off an aeroplane, annoyed with him—and she was still, by far, the most beautiful thing he'd ever seen.

'Where is home, exactly?' Luce asked as they pulled out of the airport.

'I told you about my grandmother's château?'

'That's where we're going? So—what? You're moving to France?'

Ben sighed. 'If you just wait—just a little bit—I promise I can do grand apologies and romantic gestures in style once we get there. And maybe once I've changed clothes.'

'It's not your clothes I'm worried about you changing. And I'm not interested in romantic gestures.'

She had her arms crossed over her chest, her creamy breasts pushing against the silk of her top. Were they bigger? *Not the time, Hampton.*

'Just the apology, then?'

Luce nodded. 'And I'd rather have that sooner than later.'

Ben smiled despite himself. 'No patience at all, have you?'

'Oh, I don't know. I think I've waited quite long enough.'

She had a point. 'I made a plan and everything, you know. There was a list.'

'Dolly's been telling me for weeks that plans need to be flexible. That's why we're painting the nursery yellow.'

'You and Dolly?'

'She's moved in. She's paying rent so we can fix up the house and make it baby-safe. And it means I won't have to be alone when the baby comes.'

Ben clenched his jaw. She wouldn't be alone. She shouldn't ever have thought she had to be alone. *Never mind the plan.*

'I'm sorry, Luce. For reacting the way I did.' Ben glanced across at her. She stared out of the window, intently focusing on something in the distance, or maybe on nothing at all. Either way, she wasn't looking at him, which was all Ben cared about. 'I was an idiot. I know that. Seb told me, and Dolly told me.'

'She wrote a song about how much of an idiot you are, you know.'

Ben laughed. He was starting to actually like Dolly, against the odds.

'The thing is, I knew I was wrong. I knew losing you, and our baby, would be the worst decision I ever made. I just couldn't see any way out of it.'

Now Luce looked at him, eyebrows raised, and Ben looked away and concentrated on the road again, just to avoid the anger in her gaze.

'You couldn't just say, *We'll figure it out together*?'

Ben winced. 'Apparently not. I was jet-lagged, tired, not thinking straight. But mostly I just didn't want to turn into my father.'

'You can't let your parents' marriage define your life.'

'I know. But Seb wanted me to take on this new work, travelling all the time, and I couldn't drag you and a kid around with me—hell, you'd never let me. And even if you did you'd hate it so much you'd leave me eventually. But I couldn't see myself staying in one place either. And I don't want to be one of those dads who's never around and then shows up for a couple of days in a whirlwind before disappearing again.'

'So you made all these decisions for me and our child without talking to me about it?'

Luce's words were cold and hard, and Ben turned off the *autoroute* with relief. Nearly home. If he could just get her to the château...

'I'm trying to make up for it now,' he said. 'Just give me the chance.'

Luce shook her head. 'I'm not sure that you can, Ben.'

The pain in her voice made his heart clench. 'Let me try.'

They drove the rest of the way in silence, and by the time Ben pulled up in front of the château the sky was growing dark. Grabbing her bag from the boot, he opened the door to help her out, and watched her as she stared up at the building.

'It's beautiful,' she said.

'It's nothing compared to you.' She turned to him in surprise, and he shrugged, moving away towards the front door.

'You know flattery isn't going to win this one for you?'

'It's not flattery if it's true,' Ben called back. And besides, he'd try every trick he could think of if it meant getting Luce to stay.

Inside, the château was cool and dark. The spring evening had turned chilly, and Luce wrapped her cardigan tighter around her as Ben flicked on the lights. Lamps around the walls flared into life, lighting the wide entrance hall and sweeping staircase.

'You want the tour?' Ben asked, and Luce nodded.

She followed him through the first door on the left.

'Drawing room,' Ben said, waiting while Luce looked around.

Everything looked dusty, unloved. Sheets lay over the chairs and sofas and the candlesticks and brassware were tarnished. There was none of the careful design of his hotel rooms, or even the cosy decoration of his cottage. This was somebody else's home—not Ben's. Not yet, anyway.

'When did you get here?' she asked as he led her back into the hall and through the next door.

'A week ago,' Ben said. He flipped on the light switch, revealing case after case of dusty leather books. 'Library, obviously.'

'You flew straight here the day after I told you?'

'I had work to do.'

Of course. For someone who said he didn't want to turn into his father, Ben seemed to be doing his damnedest to become exactly the same sort of workaholic.

He led her across the hallway to show her a front sitting room and a formal dining room. More antique furniture, more dustsheets. More floral wallpaper and heavy curtains.

'This place doesn't seem very *you*,' she commented.

'It isn't yet. Lot of work to do.'

'Is that why you came straight here as soon as you got back from your work trip? Or is there a hotel nearby you're looking at acquiring?'

'Always with the questions…' Ben took her arm, tucking her hand into the crook of his arm just as he had that night in Chester. 'Come see the kitchen, then I'll explain everything.'

The kitchen stretched across the back of the house, with huge full-length windows leading out to the garden. The units were old and battered, but Luce could see what a fabulous space it could be, redone properly. The whole house had huge potential. Small for a château, she supposed, but plenty big enough for any modern family.

Not that she would be moving to France, of course. Ben hadn't even suggested it. In fact she had no idea at all what he wanted from her.

'It's a lovely kitchen,' she said, rounding on him. 'Now, talk.'

Ben smiled, and the love in his eyes as he looked at her shocked her. He looked...open. Free.

'I spoke to Seb,' he started. 'The morning after I saw you. Told him what an idiot I'd been. Told him I couldn't see how I could fix it—having you and a family—with my job. But without the job I couldn't support you, and being stuck in an office five days a week would drive me crazy.'

'I know that. I'd never ask you to do that.' Luce pulled away from him. 'I told you—you don't have to be involved if you don't want to be. But why you dragged me out here to tell me this again—'

'I didn't,' Ben said, grabbing her hands. 'Just listen—please. Actually, come upstairs with me.'

'Only if you talk as we go,' Luce said, hating the burning tears she could feel forming in her eyes. Damn hormones. They confused everything. She just wanted answers. No need to get upset.

'Okay,' Ben said with a laugh. 'You've been very patient with me.'

Holding her hand, he walked them back into the hallway and up the staircase.

'Seb asked me what I really wanted,' he said. 'And I realised it was the same question I'd kept asking you. You hadn't been able to answer it. But suddenly I could. The only thing in the world I wanted that morning, and every morning since, was you in my life. You and our child. No one-night rules. No running away. Just you. Always. However you'll have me.'

Luce looked up in surprise and the stair carpet slipped under her foot. Ben wrapped a strong arm around her waist and she grabbed at his shoulders as she found her balance and tried to get her heartbeat back under control.

Ben smiled at her, carrying on as if nothing had happened. 'So Seb ordered coffee, and we worked out a plan to make it all work. A long-term, lasting plan. You'd have been so proud of us.'

'I already am,' Luce murmured. He'd made the right choice. It had taken him a couple of days, maybe, but he'd chosen to stay, to fight. Chosen responsibility and grown-up life over running away like a teenager. 'So, what was the plan?'

'We tackled work first, because I was so worried about making the same mistakes Dad did. I offered to quit, but Seb had a better plan. I'm going to keep developing our new hotel line—family-friendly, boutique business ho-tels—but I'm going to get help to do it. You can come with me, whenever you want, and we'll structure it so I'm not away more than two weeks in every month.'

Luce blinked. 'So—wait. You want to be with me—with us—when you're in the country?'

Ben grinned and pulled her up the rest of the stairs. 'I love you, Luce. I want to be with you all the time. Did I miss that part out?'

'Yes.'

'Well, I do. I want to be a real family with you. And I know now what a real family needs.'

'What's that?'

'A home. Or, in our case, several.' He threw open a door off the landing and Luce looked in to see sunny yellow walls and boxes of nursery furniture piled in the centre of the room. 'I'd hoped to get at least the crib put together be-fore you arrived. Painting took longer than I remembered.'

Luce bit her lip. 'You want us to live here?' That would mean leaving Dolly—and Tom and Mum. Leaving Cardiff. Leaving her job. Giving up everything she loved. Would he really ask her to do that?

'Sometimes.' Ben wrapped his arms around her waist and pulled her against him. 'I figure we'll fix up your Cardiff house and live there most of the time. I mean, I don't imagine you're going to want to suddenly give up your home and your work or anything, but we can spend summers here at the château.'

Hope flared up inside her. Maybe he did understand after all. 'And any time we need a weekend to get away from it all we can go to the cottage?'

'Exactly.'

Ben smiled down at her and Luce tried to remember if she'd ever seen him looking so happy. She didn't think so. Not even after making love.

It all sounded perfect. More than she'd ever hoped or dreamed for. To be with him, just their little family, all the time. Except... 'I told you Dolly moved in, right?'

'I don't care. As long as I get to be with you. Besides, we might need a babysitter.'

Luce laughed. 'Very true.'

'So you'll do it?' Ben asked. 'You'll take the chance that I've changed? Grown up?'

Luce smiled up at him. 'I love you, you idiot. Of course I will.'

Ben lowered his lips to hers and kissed her softly. 'That's okay, then.'

'Well, seeing the château did make a bit of a difference. And I like the idea of homes in two countries...'

Ben shook his head. 'That's what I realised. These buildings aren't home. *You* are. You and our baby. That's home to me.'

Luce's shoulders relaxed as she tucked her head against his chest. That was what she'd needed to hear.

Things weren't just going to be okay any more, she knew. Their life together would be magnificent.

\* \* \* \* \*

# Mills & Boon® Hardback
## September 2013

## ROMANCE

| | |
|---|---|
| Challenging Dante | Lynne Graham |
| Captivated by Her Innocence | Kim Lawrence |
| Lost to the Desert Warrior | Sarah Morgan |
| His Unexpected Legacy | Chantelle Shaw |
| Never Say No to a Caffarelli | Melanie Milburne |
| His Ring Is Not Enough | Maisey Yates |
| A Reputation to Uphold | Victoria Parker |
| A Whisper of Disgrace | Sharon Kendrick |
| If You Can't Stand the Heat... | Joss Wood |
| Maid of Dishonour | Heidi Rice |
| Bound by a Baby | Kate Hardy |
| In the Line of Duty | Ami Weaver |
| Patchwork Family in the Outback | Soraya Lane |
| Stranded with the Tycoon | Sophie Pembroke |
| The Rebound Guy | Fiona Harper |
| Greek for Beginners | Jackie Braun |
| A Child to Heal Their Hearts | Dianne Drake |
| Sheltered by Her Top-Notch Boss | Joanna Neil |

## MEDICAL

| | |
|---|---|
| The Wife He Never Forgot | Anne Fraser |
| The Lone Wolf's Craving | Tina Beckett |
| Re-awakening His Shy Nurse | Annie Claydon |
| Safe in His Hands | Amy Ruttan |

0813 GEN STD HB

## *Mills & Boon® Large Print*
### *September 2013*

# ROMANCE

| | |
|---|---|
| **A Rich Man's Whim** | Lynne Graham |
| **A Price Worth Paying?** | Trish Morey |
| **A Touch of Notoriety** | Carole Mortimer |
| **The Secret Casella Baby** | Cathy Williams |
| **Maid for Montero** | Kim Lawrence |
| **Captive in his Castle** | Chantelle Shaw |
| **Heir to a Dark Inheritance** | Maisey Yates |
| **Anything but Vanilla...** | Liz Fielding |
| **A Father for Her Triplets** | Susan Meier |
| **Second Chance with the Rebel** | Cara Colter |
| **First Comes Baby...** | Michelle Douglas |

# HISTORICAL

| | |
|---|---|
| **The Greatest of Sins** | Christine Merrill |
| **Tarnished Amongst the Ton** | Louise Allen |
| **The Beauty Within** | Marguerite Kaye |
| **The Devil Claims a Wife** | Helen Dickson |
| **The Scarred Earl** | Elizabeth Beacon |

# MEDICAL

| | |
|---|---|
| **NYC Angels: Redeeming The Playboy** | Carol Marinelli |
| **NYC Angels: Heiress's Baby Scandal** | Janice Lynn |
| **St Piran's: The Wedding!** | Alison Roberts |
| **Sydney Harbour Hospital: Evie's Bombshell** | Amy Andrews |
| **The Prince Who Charmed Her** | Fiona McArthur |
| **His Hidden American Beauty** | Connie Cox |

# ROMANCE

| | |
|---|---|
| The Greek's Marriage Bargain | Sharon Kendrick |
| An Enticing Debt to Pay | Annie West |
| The Playboy of Puerto Banús | Carol Marinelli |
| Marriage Made of Secrets | Maya Blake |
| Never Underestimate a Caffarelli | Melanie Milburne |
| The Divorce Party | Jennifer Hayward |
| A Hint of Scandal | Tara Pammi |
| A Façade to Shatter | Lynn Raye Harris |
| Whose Bed Is It Anyway? | Natalie Anderson |
| Last Groom Standing | Kimberly Lang |
| Single Dad's Christmas Miracle | Susan Meier |
| Snowbound with the Soldier | Jennifer Faye |
| The Redemption of Rico D'Angelo | Michelle Douglas |
| The Christmas Baby Surprise | Shirley Jump |
| Backstage with Her Ex | Louisa George |
| Blame It on the Champagne | Nina Harrington |
| Christmas Magic in Heatherdale | Abigail Gordon |
| The Motherhood Mix-Up | Jennifer Taylor |

# MEDICAL

| | |
|---|---|
| Gold Coast Angels: A Doctor's Redemption | Marion Lennox |
| Gold Coast Angels: Two Tiny Heartbeats | Fiona McArthur |
| The Secret Between Them | Lucy Clark |
| Craving Her Rough Diamond Doc | Amalie Berlin |

# *Mills & Boon® Large Print*
## *October 2013*

# ROMANCE

| | |
|---|---|
| **The Sheikh's Prize** | Lynne Graham |
| **Forgiven but not Forgotten?** | Abby Green |
| **His Final Bargain** | Melanie Milburne |
| **A Throne for the Taking** | Kate Walker |
| **Diamond in the Desert** | Susan Stephens |
| **A Greek Escape** | Elizabeth Power |
| **Princess in the Iron Mask** | Victoria Parker |
| **The Man Behind the Pinstripes** | Melissa McClone |
| **Falling for the Rebel Falcon** | Lucy Gordon |
| **Too Close for Comfort** | Heidi Rice |
| **The First Crush Is the Deepest** | Nina Harrington |

# HISTORICAL

| | |
|---|---|
| **Reforming the Viscount** | Annie Burrows |
| **A Reputation for Notoriety** | Diane Gaston |
| **The Substitute Countess** | Lyn Stone |
| **The Sword Dancer** | Jeannie Lin |
| **His Lady of Castlemora** | Joanna Fulford |

# MEDICAL

| | |
|---|---|
| **NYC Angels: Unmasking Dr Serious** | Laura Iding |
| **NYC Angels: The Wallflower's Secret** | Susan Carlisle |
| **Cinderella of Harley Street** | Anne Fraser |
| **You, Me and a Family** | Sue MacKay |
| **Their Most Forbidden Fling** | Melanie Milburne |
| **The Last Doctor She Should Ever Date** | Louisa George |